Devlin's Dare

A Tryst Island Erotic Romance

SABRINA YORK

Karen

Keep it <u>hot</u>

Sabrina York

DEDICATION

This book is dedicated to Delilah Devlin, Lisa Fox, Vanessa Romano and Tara Sheets. When you read the book, you'll know why, if you don't already.

ACKNOWLEDGMENTS

First of all, thanks to my amazing beta readers, Carmen Cook, Angie Lane, Tina LaRue, Tina Reiter, and Fedora. And to my amazing street team— Charmaine Arredondo, Crystal Benedict, Crystal Biby, Kris Bloom, Kim Brown, Sandy Butler, Jodi Ciorciari Marinich, Celeste Deveney, Tracey A. Diczban, Shelly Estes, Stephanie Felix, Joany Kane, C. Morgan Kennedy, Angie Lane, Tina LaRue, Rose Lipscomb, Chris Lewis, Kathleen Mixon, Laurie Peterson, Tina Reiter, Hollie Rieth, Regina Ross, Dee Thomas, Sheri Vidal and Michelle Wilson, as well as the shy ones, Christy, Elf, Fedora, Gaele, Hotcha, Laurie, Pansy Petal and Rae—for their support of my books and writing. Many of them provided the naughty ideas for Tara and Devlin's dares.

My deepest appreciation to Wicked Smart Designs for a rocking cover— always gorgeous—and to Monica Britt for helping me whip this novella into shape.

My heartfelt appreciation to my fellow writers for their support. Especially Kayelle Allen, Avery Aster, Emily Cale, Cassandra Carr, Margie Church, Cerise DeLand, Delilah Devlin, Adrienne deWolfe, Laurann Dohner, Tina Donahue, Lisa Fox, Gabrielle Holly, Desiree Holt, Adriana Kraft, Kathy Kulig, Eloreen Moon, Nicole Morgan, Beverly Ovalle, Zenobia Renquist and Bernadette Walsh.

To all my friends in the Greater Seattle Romance Writers of America, Passionate Ink and Rose City Romance Writers groups, thank you for all your support and encouragement.

CHAPTER ONE

Tara Romano hurried up the narrow stairs toward the galley of the ferry, hunting in her purse for her phone. Damn it all. Where was it—

The air gushed out of her lungs as she turned the corner and plowed into a stone wall.

No. Not a stone wall. A chest as hard as stone.

She bounced off and reeled back. Panic flooded her as she teetered on the brink of the platform. Strong hands grabbed her arms, keeping her from tumbling down the narrow staircase. She gasped and clutched at her savior. "Thank you…" But the words caught in her throat. Her heart seized as she looked up into the bluest eyes she'd ever seen. They crinkled at the corners as he smiled and her attention flickered to his lips.

Brain freeze.

Holy Hannah, this was one cute guy. Sculpted, tanned features, a blade-like nose and short, spiky, nut-brown hair. And his body—*lord have mercy*. This close, she had the perfect view of his chin. It was bold and square and covered with a hint of golden brown fuzz.

Something in her belly fluttered.

She loved fuzz on a guy. She loved bold square chins. She was tempted to nibble, but resisted the urge.

The wind whipped through the girders and gusted into her. The boat lunged. She teetered again.

His grip on her tightened. Heat seared her at his touch. And fantasies? They seared her as well. Hot, steamy visions of the two of them entwined in—

"Careful," he said, his voice low and laced with humor. He stepped back and eased her onto the narrow platform. "It's choppy."

Tara blinked. "Hmm?" Yeah. Words. Not flowing.

"The sea. It's picking up. You might want to go inside." He pushed open the door to the inner deck, stepping back so she could pass.

"Oh. Right." Why her mood dipped was a mystery. He was only being polite. The wind had kicked up, and with it, the chop of the sea.

But it had been nice, being melded against his chest for a moment. A brief moment. A flash of time.

Pressed against that hard warmth.

Drawing the scent of him deep into her lungs…

Yeah. She probably needed to get laid. Since she'd given Chet the heave-ho, her love life had been rather sparse. It was her choice, and it was a damn good choice. Right now she needed, above all things, to focus on salvaging her failing business. Men were a distraction. Relationships, an annoyance. She had no business thinking about this man, much less fantasizing about doing wicked things with him.

But it had been a while. Too long, maybe, judging from the ache in her womb.

She sucked in a deep breath and firmed her resolve. "Thank you," she said, dipping her head to hide her raging blush. Good lord, she'd practically curled herself around him, right there on the surging platform, and *tasted* his chin.

She readjusted her purse, patted down her wind-blown hair and entered the inner deck of the boat, trying very hard not to glance over her shoulder at that Greek God.

She failed.

That he was still standing there, holding the door, and watching her walk away—more specifically, with his eyes glued to her ass—was a balm to her ego. He looked up and caught her staring at him. His lips quirked into a wicked grin.

And he winked.

She-it.

Devlin Fox let the heavy door close on the vision, but it was damn

2

tough. He'd seen her earlier, boarding the ferry with a group of friends. They'd all been drop dead gorgeous, but this one, this petite angel with long brown hair caught up in a swishy ponytail, had snagged his attention. Her laugh, something wild and musical, had curled around his gut like a fist, and yanked.

And then, to have her come bouncing up the stairs—not watching where she was going and utterly unaware of exactly how much she was *bouncing*—and plow right into him... It had been breathtaking.

She'd felt divine plastered against his body from tits to groin and though it had only been for a second, he had no doubt it was burned on his memory forever.

The ferry only had one stop left, so he knew where she was going, and excitement scudded in his veins.

She was heading to Tryst Island. She'd probably be there the whole weekend.

Surely that was enough time for a seduction.

And he was between flings. Perfect timing.

He bounded down the stairs to the car deck, fishing his keys from his pocket. He'd left his tablet in the trunk, which had been stupid. Whenever he left his tablet, he had ideas. And this one had been brilliant. Though, at the moment, he had to struggle to remember what that brilliant idea had been. His collision with a little slice of heaven had wiped it from his mind entirely. But then, ah, yes, he remembered.

The béarnaise had been flogged like a slave and drizzled over limp asparagus desperate to escape the plate.

The perfect description for the entrée he'd suffered through last night at a new frou frou eatery.

Too much?

Probably not.

It had been a dismal meal.

Anticipation swirled. He loved when the meals were dismal. It made his job as an irreverent food critic much more interesting.

Writing good reviews wasn't nearly as much fun.

Of course, he'd made a lot of enemies with his review blog. Likely, at some point, he wouldn't be able to get a meal in Seattle at all...unless he wore a disguise. But people weren't interested in good reviews. At least, not judging from the comments on his postings.

Judging from the comments on his postings, people loved snark.

And the snarkier, the better.

Fortunately, Devlin Fox excelled at snark.

Especially when it referenced execrable edibles. Or pretentious presentation. Or substandard service.

Last night's meal had been all three. He was aflame with ideas for this review. Literally. Aflame.

He grinned to himself as he wove his way to the car and grabbed his tablet, stopping to tap in a few of his more pithy observations right there on the car deck. One never knew where inspiration could strike, and it paid to capture a thought while the ember glowed bright.

And it paid well.

It had never been his intention to be a food critic. In fact, he'd diligently studied literature with every intention of becoming a bestselling author of critically acclaimed fiction. Life had intruded on that aspiration in the form of his friend Christopher Moss who, over drinks one night, had been impressed by Devlin's diatribe on a dingy hole-in-the-wall Chinese restaurant featuring egg foo yong Frisbees and pot stickers that could double as hockey pucks. Chris had appreciated the sports references and offered Devlin a job writing occasional reviews for his Seattle Spotlight Magazine.

His column was an instant hit with the hipsters, the grungers, and the local tech nerds teeming in the region. It quickly morphed into a standalone blog on Chris' website with a following of over two hundred thousand fans, many of whom didn't even live in Seattle.

Even though he enjoyed the success of this accidental career, he still dreamed of writing that novel. But honestly, there was no time.

He refused to contemplate the bubbling fear that his imaginary novel might not be as successful as his rants on desiccated chicken breasts and greasy-haired servers beset with the winds.

With a sigh, he headed back up the stairs to the main deck, thrusting all thoughts of his ridiculous pipe dream from his head, and focusing on his review of La Boucherie, home of desperate asparagus, curdled béarnaise and prime rib so undercooked it was still chewing its cud.

He slipped into the booth he and his friends Parker and Richie had staked out in the ferry cafeteria—though those two were nowhere to be seen at the moment—and tapped in a few more notes. Then he pulled out his cell phone, quickly flicking through his messages. He did that often, as he composed in his head. The cell phone required little concentration. Without much thought at all, he deleted texts from Ann and Marjie and Alice, none of whom seemed able to grasp the concept that it was over. But he kept the naked picture of Shayla. Strictly for sentimental reasons.

He was thinking about those reasons, smiling a little crookedly, when Parker pushed in from the outer deck and plopped into his seat with a shudder.

"It's cold out there."

"Dude. It's summer." Devlin looked out the wide windows at the ice-blue waters of the Sound, the bird's egg sky flecked with puffy white clouds. It wasn't often sunny in the Pacific Northwest, but when God decided to make a nice day, he made a damn fine one.

"I know." Parker pulled on his jacket. "But it's windy."

Devlin eyed his friend. He wasn't skinny, *per se*, but he could gain a little weight. "Maybe you need to eat a burger."

Parker snorted at the running joke. "Yeah. I read your review of Ferry Food."

"It's not all bad…"

"Hmm. I believe someone once said, *There's a reason they sell beer and wine in ferry cafeterias.*"

The two shared a grin. He and Parker had known each other since they'd pledged the same frat in college. Over the years, their casual acquaintance had deepened into friendship. Parker was a stand up guy. Dependable. Decent.

Parker never talked about his past, and Devlin never asked, but he knew there had been some dark moments. The mark on his cheek— the exact size and shape of a man's ring—was nearly unnoticeable, but the mottled scars on his neck, peeping over the turtleneck he always wore, spoke to a shitload of anguish. Devlin knew the pain he carried within was worse.

Everyone in Parker's family had died when he was a boy. Though he was now a successful lawyer for a large Seattle law firm, it was only because Adam Bristol, their friend Ash's dad, had taken him under his wing.

"Well, the coffee's good…" Devlin offered. "And the pastries are almost fresh."

Parker snorted a laugh. "Almost fresh. Devlin, you do have a way with words."

"Yeah." He glanced back down at his phone. "That's what they say." The inconvenient desire to write something meaningful and important rose again and Devlin pushed it down. Restaurant reviews were plenty meaningful enough. People had to eat, after all. And, come to think of it, so did he.

And the money was good. Artists starved, didn't they?

"What a world. What a world." Richie threw himself into the seat next to Parker. A cloud of alcoholic vapor, twined with stultifying cologne, wafted around him.

Parker waved his hand in front of his face. "Holy crap, Richie. What have you been drinking?"

Richie pulled out a flask and waggled it. "Vodka. Want some?"

"No," Parker said on a laugh. "Isn't it a little early?"

"S'never too early to start drinking my friend!" Richie tipped to the side and clapped Parker on the shoulder. It took him a moment to right himself.

Devlin and Parker exchanged a glance. When Richie drank, he *drank*. They'd probably have to carry him to Ash's house. Which was a charming thought. Because Richie stank. It wasn't that he didn't use deodorant. Unfortunately, a deodorant strong enough to cover his manfunk had not yet been invented. The cologne he bathed in didn't help matters.

Richie wasn't Devlin's favorite person, but Ash had invited him to spend the weekend at his house on the island, so they were stuck with him. At least for the weekend. Devlin fixated on the ascot Richie had tied jauntily around his neck. Richie was the kind of guy who couldn't simply be what he was. He always needed to pretend to be more.

Apparently he thought lots of jewelry and an ascot marked him as a wealthy playboy.

Devlin knew several wealthy playboys. None of them wore ascots.

"Didja see those hot foxes?" Richie nodded to the far corner of the cafeteria. The effort nearly tipped him over again.

Devlin turned in that direction and stilled. His mouth went dry as he set eyes on *her*. Damn, she was fine. She shook her head and her ponytail swished. He didn't know why it affected him the way it did, that ponytail. He wanted to grab it, wrap it around his fist, and hold on.

That vision swamped him. Only in his vision, they were both

naked. She was before him on her hands and knees and he had a tight grip on the reins and was sinking in deep…

Yeah. A boner this hard should be illegal in public.

He was about to look away—really, he was—when she turned her head and their gazes clashed. He thought he saw her smile, a mere twitch of those rosy lips. He thought he saw a delicate blush creep up her cheeks.

She was all the way across the deck. He was probably only imagining things.

But hell, he had a damn fine imagination.

He was definitely—*definitely*—going to have to find her this weekend.

And seduce her.

He could do it. He had a way with words. Everyone said so.

And women loved him.

Oh yeah. He would have her this weekend. No doubt about it.

CHAPTER TWO

Tara couldn't hold back a grin when she walked into Darby's Bar and Grill with Emily, Jamie and Kaitlin, who had come over with her on the ferry. Kristi lit up at the sight of her and waved. It felt like coming home.

She wasn't sure why.

Tara had never gone to college, choosing instead to attend culinary school. She'd never regretted her decision, but in her heart of hearts, she'd always been a little jealous of her friend Kristi and her tight camaraderie with the Dawgs. Early on in her college days at the University of Washington, Kristi had had the good fortune to be assigned to McCarty Hall where she'd met the most amazing group of friends. For four years the Dawgs, as they called themselves, had banded together, helping each other study, survive and snag the big screen TV in the lounge for marathon football binges.

Once they'd all graduated, they'd continued to hang out, even sharing a vacation house on an island populated by Seattle's rich and privileged.

Tara felt blessed whenever they invited her to hang out with them. And a little sad that this tribe wasn't really *hers*.

What Tara envied the most was the relationships. The men in the group were like overly protective brothers and the women like soul sisters. They always—always—stuck up for each other, often like rabid pit bulls. She'd craved friendships like these; her life had been fraught with upheaval, moving every year or so as a child. She treasured the times when she was included in the group—the odd weekend here and there. But deep in her soul, she knew she wasn't "one of them."

As she approached the table, something snagged her attention and her steps stalled.

Holy shit. Cam had his arm around Kristi. And it wasn't a casual *gee-where-should-I-put-my-arm* embrace. It was a *she-is-mine-so-fuck-you-all* embrace.

Tara swallowed the painful lump in her throat and forced a smile. The bright light of Kristi's response nearly blinded her. Kristi had always had the hots for Cam. How many thousands of times had Tara been forced to listen to her woeful longings? Of course, she'd ended each conversation with a panicked *please don't tell anyone.*

And now, here they sat, plain as day.

A couple.

Yeah. Envy was a horrible thing.

And the strange thing was, Tara wasn't even sure why she was jealous. She didn't want a man. Didn't need a relationship—in fact she had vowed to avoid them. She certainly didn't have those kinds of feelings for Cam.

She should be happy for Kristi.

She resolved to work on that.

Taking her seat, her gaze fell on Kristi's sister Bella and, once again, her brain hiccupped. Because Holt Lamm, the beast, the biggest, bossiest man in the group, had his arm around *her* shoulders. Bella, the prickliest woman on the planet, now had a *boyfriend.*

What the hell was going on here?

Clearly, the universe was mocking her. Or punishing her for dumping a perfectly adequate man simply because he didn't thrill her to the core.

Or punishing her by mocking her.

First that up-close and personal run-in with a super hot guy, and now two of her long-time single friends were paired up with guys they'd always drooled over—though in Bella's case, the drooling had been clandestine. But Tara had noticed.

Regardless, it wasn't nice of the universe to mock her like that.

Kaitlin slid a menu over the polished wood of the table and Tara slid it right on over to Jamie. She already knew what she was ordering. She always had the same thing when she came here. Darby had an amazing blue cheese and apple salad with walnuts and creamy vinaigrette. It was something she dreamed about and drooled over when she wasn't here.

Silence settled around the table as everyone else studied the menus. It was shattered when a loud thud, followed by a cheer, resounded through the room. Tara glanced over toward the ruckus and her nose wrinkled as she recognized the guy with the ascot from the ferry wallowing in the sawdust next to his overturned chair. *Idiot.*

He'd been drunk off his ass when he'd cornered her on the car deck, precipitating her headlong flight up the stairs and into the arms of—

Her heart stuttered as her attention landed on *him.*

He was smiling a bit as he reached out a hand to the idiot on the floor. She allowed herself a second, or maybe more, to soak in his gorgeousness. It should be against the law for one man to be so dang cute.

"Who are those guys?" she asked. She didn't mean to ask. The words slipped out through the drool.

"The blond is Ash Bristol," Holt responded—though it had been a rhetorical question. "He has the place next to ours."

"Bristol?" Emily peeped. "As in the Bristol Foundation?"

Cam nodded. "Ash is the 'heir apparent.'" He took a sip of his beer. "Ash is a friend of Lane's." Their friend, Lane Daniels, another one of the Dawgs, owned the vacation house they shared.

"And the others?" Tara asked, because really, Ash was not the one whose name she needed to know.

Cam smirked. "I don't know the guy in the ascot." Snorts around the table at that. "But that's Parker Rieth in the blue and Devlin Fox in the Polo shirt."

Tara's heart stopped. And then began thudding painfully in her temples as a white hot fury overcame her. "*That's* Devlin Fox?" She glared across the restaurant. It wasn't bad enough that the gorgeous guy she ran into on the ferry turned out to be friends with the douche in the ascot she'd been running from. No.

He had to be her worst enemy too.

Damn. Damn damn damn.

"You know him?" Bella asked.

"He writes a Foodie Blog." Tara glowered around the table, trying hard not to snarl. Or pout. "He gave Stud Muffin a bad review."

"What?" Cam squawked.

Jamie shook her head. "Why did he do that?"

Tara crossed her arms over her chest. She'd spent her life learning her craft. Spent her life savings opening her own bakery. Spent years building clientele. Then, with one crappy review, business had tanked. Totally into the toilet. In one fell swoop, many of her regulars had stopped coming in.

She wasn't sure she'd be able to make the bills this month, which was devastating.

And all because of *him*.

It was unfair for one man to have so much power.

And why had he panned her bakery? "Because I don't have gluten-free," she muttered, then added, under her breath, "Big baby."

Still, gluten-free was a huge deal in Seattle. She'd spent the past week working up recipes. And fantasizing about wreaking vengeance on a certain blogger.

It had been a mere fantasy, until now. But now...

Kaitlin shifted closer, drawing Tara's attention. "What are you thinking?" she asked in a whisper, her features tight.

Tara froze. It didn't do to think around Kaitlin. Not that the elfin redhead read minds, or at least that's what she claimed. But she seemed to *know* things.

"Nothing." Tara made it a point to bat her lashes.

Kaitlin's nose rumpled, as though she smelled something nasty. Like a lie.

But hell. Tara couldn't tell Kaitlin what she was really thinking because Kaitlin—the sweet, innocent soul that she was—would try to talk her out of it. Ramble on about Karma and shit.

No, Tara couldn't tell anyone what she was really thinking about.

Because she was plotting revenge.

She was going to get Devlin Fox back. And she was going to get him good.

"Hi there."

Devlin turned on the barstool, where he was waiting for a drink, his trademark smile firmly in place. Everything within him froze. It was her. That little slice of heaven from the ferry. Damn. She was as hot as he remembered.

She sidled up next to him and the chatter of the bar receded.

Fascination—and something else—rose.

"Well, hello there."

He liked her scent, something floral and light. He liked her heat as she pressed against his side. She lowered her long lush lashes and peeped up at him through the fringe. Damn, that was sexy. She licked her lips. That was sexy too.

"I never got to thank you," she purred.

"Th-Thank me?" Was that her hand? On his thigh?

Shit yeah.

"For saving me." Her fingers flexed. "I would have tumbled to my death if you hadn't grabbed me."

"I doubt you would have tumbled to your death. Disfigurement, perhaps. Dire injury. But not death. Don't exaggerate."

She laughed, a low chortle. "Well… Thank you." She leaned closer and whispered, "Can I buy you a drink?"

Devlin blinked. He'd been hit on in bars before, but no woman had ever offered to buy him a drink.

She might just be a perfect woman. "Sure."

"What's your poison?"

"Whiskey sour."

She signaled to the bartender.

"So…I'm Devlin."

"Devlin." She cooed. Actually cooed.

"And you are…?"

"Interested."

He jumped a little as her hand skated up his thigh. His pulse skipped. "I…ah…yes. But what can I call you?" He had a pretty good idea where this was headed, and he wanted to know what to cry out as he sank into her steamy depths. It was only polite to know a woman's name at a moment like that.

She pursed her lips, as though she were thinking it over. Or thinking about something else. Her thumb snaked up. Nudged his balls, ever so lightly, and through thick denim, but he felt it like an electrical charge. "Call me Sugar."

"Sugar." Oh yeah. She was sweet.

"Would you…like to go for a walk?"

"A walk?" His cock lurched. All thoughts of that drink faded.

"It's a beautiful night…"

She looked over her shoulder and then threaded her fingers in his, leading him toward the back of the bar. He didn't know why they weren't heading for the front door, but didn't much care.

She was a beautiful woman. She wanted him. And he was just drunk enough to follow her anywhere she led.

He shot a glance at Parker who sent him a thumbs up.

They barely made it out the back door of the bar before she kissed him. Damn. Backed him up against the wall, raked her fingers through his hair, pulled his head down and took his mouth.

And damn, she was a good kisser. She ate him with heat and passion and carnivorous zeal. He responded in kind, thrusting his tongue into her mouth. He nearly passed out when she sucked on it, nibbled it, toyed with it. He couldn't help imagining her doing the same to his cock.

Her palm roved over his chest and made its way down to his hips. He didn't dare move as she slowly teased the band of his jeans. She pulled back and held his gaze as she popped the snap.

"Mmm," she murmured, reaching in. His eyes crossed as she molded his length. Squeezed. "Such a big boy." She licked her lips and his brain short-circuited. When she went to her knees before him and blew a hot breath on him through the cotton of his briefs, he nearly lost consciousness. "I want to taste you," she said. "Take off your pants."

Holy God. Yes.

In a frenzy, he kicked off his shoes, and ripped off his jeans, hopping from one foot to the other. He held still, frozen in place, as she hooked her thumbs in his briefs and eased them down revealing his eager cock. She dragged his underwear down until they pooled at his ankles.

He heard the catch in her moan. Felt the trace of a warm finger around his swollen head and down to the base. He shuddered.

"Ah. Yes," she said, coming close. Her heat caressed him. His knees knocked. She fisted him. Pumped. Once. Twice. Blood pounded at his temples. Thrummed in his cock. She bent closer. Her damp breath kissed the head. "Such a big dick," she said.

If he'd been in his right mind, her tone would have warned him, but he wasn't in his right mind. He was a little drunk and a lot horny and there was a gorgeous woman on her knees before him with his cock in her fist. Her mouth hovered over the tip.

Yes. Yes. Just a little more…

She released him and stood up in a rush. Her beautiful, seductive expression morphed into something bitter. He gaped at her, stunned.

"Yeah," she said, propping her fists on her hips. "You, Devlin Fox, are a big dick."

And then she left. Whirled on her heel and left him standing there, half-naked, leaning against the grimy brick wall behind a grungy bar.

And she took his jeans.

CHAPTER THREE

He would, until the end of time, feel grateful to Charmaine, Darby's perky little waitress.

She came upon him as he hunkered behind the dumpster, desperately trying to decide what to do. He could sprint back to the house hoping to hell no one would see him, or dig through the trash in hopes of finding something to cover himself.

He'd never been terribly shy about his body, but there was something about being totally exposed behind a bar—with an epic hard on, after having been mercilessly teased by a gorgeous vixen—that left a man feeling mauled and vulnerable.

One thought bubbled in his brain.

He was going to have to pay her back for this.

Charmaine stopped short when she saw him skulking there, hunched over, pulling his t-shirt down to cover his junk. He could only imagine what she thought, though her expression was fairly telling.

"I'm not a perv," he said, the first words to trip from his tongue.

She tipped her head to the side and her lips quirked. "Really?"

Heat flooded his face and prickled his nape. "She stole my jeans."

"She?" He could tell the waitress was struggling to hold back a laugh.

"Please… Could you help me?"

Maybe his tone was sufficiently penitent, or maybe she'd simply seen it all and wanted to get this naked guy out of her trash bin, but she relented. "I'll find you something."

He hated watching her walk away, suddenly noticing a cool breeze coming in off the dark ocean. Goosebumps rose on his skin. A shiver racked him. But she returned in due course with a pair of folded sweats. They were a couple sizes too large, but he pulled them on and tugged the drawstring, feeling like a warrior girding his loins for battle. "Thank you," he muttered.

She snorted a laugh. "Sure. Anytime." Still chuckling, she went back inside.

Devlin made a note to give her a phenomenal tip the next time he visited the bar. Which, he suspected, might not be for a while. He didn't relish the thought of seeing *her* again.

At least, not until he had plotted his revenge.

Thank God none of the guys had been around when he arrived home wearing some other dude's sweatpants. He could only imagine the razzing he'd take over that.

He didn't hide out for the rest of the weekend. At least that's what he told himself. But he certainly didn't go back to the bar. And though he swore not to think about her, he couldn't help himself.

There was something about her he just couldn't get out of his mind. Sure, she was gorgeous. Of all her friends, she was the one who caught and held his attention. Her features, so delicate and piquant, her long ponytail, her curves.

He'd always loved pranks, and pranksters. But no one had ever gotten the better of him...until her.

When he and his friends boarded the ferry on Sunday afternoon, she was there with her coterie. Their eyes met across the breadth of the main cabin and she grinned at him. But it wasn't a friendly grin.

It was an evil grin.

Determination formed a ball in his gut.

Determination for revenge.

He wanted that woman. Beneath him. Around him. Encompassing him.

It was a damn shame he didn't know her name.

Tara shivered as she leaned against the rail of the ferry, staring out at the dull gray choppy water. Flecks of white tipped the tiny waves and wind-kissed ripples swirled. It was a gloomy day for summer on the Sound. Gunmetal clouds skirted the sun and an impenetrable fog wreathed the passing islands. But it matched her mood.

He was inside.

What were the odds they'd both catch the same ferry home?

Pretty good, apparently.

It wasn't bad enough that she hadn't been able to get him out of her mind all weekend. That he'd haunted her every thought. Wasn't bad enough that she had freaking *dreamed* about him…about his trusting, hopeful smile, his scent, the weight of his cock in her hand.

There was no reason for her for feel guilt over what she did. Certainly no reason for regret.

He was a bastard of epic proportions. A heartless, soulless husk of a man with no conscience and no moral compass whatsoever. He blatantly ruined worlds with the slash of a pen. Or the tap of a key. Whatever.

Point was, he'd deserved it.

This churning acid in her gut, the slow burn of remorse, was utterly unwarranted.

She sucked in a deep breath and tipped her gaze up to the sky, watching the gulls wheel in their wake. Tiny sprinkles, too small to be called raindrops cooled her cheeks.

Why did he have to be on *this* ferry?

"It's raining."

Tara blinked and turned to smile at Kristi as she sidled up next to her. It wasn't a terribly sincere smile. But it was the effort that counted. "Not so much. Besides, I like it."

"Hmm." Kristi leaned against the rail and turned her attention to the frothing foam churned up by the rear propellers. There was something soothing about standing on the stern of the boat, surveying where you'd been. It wasn't as exhilarating as standing on the bow, facing the adventure with the wind whipping your face until tears formed, but sometimes one needed soothing. "Tara?"

"Yeah?" Another ferry appeared in the distance, a mere dot on the horizon. A flash of sliver caught her eye—A surfacing salmon? A fluke?—but it was gone before she turned her head.

"Is everything okay?"

Tara's heart stuttered. *Shit.* The last thing she wanted was to talk about *everything* with Kristi. "Sure."

"You've been… I dunno, kinda quiet this weekend. Is everything okay with Chet?"

"Yeah. Well." Tara blew out a breath. "Chet and I kind of broke up."

"Oh, no." She didn't expect a hug. Didn't deserve one. "Did he dump you?"

It was all Tara could do not to send her friend a sarcastic look. Nobody ever dumped Tara Romano. She was the one who did the dumping.

Not because she was a serial dumper. She wasn't. It was just that, when she was in a relationship with a guy, he would invariably become too possessive. Boxing her in. Making her feel trapped.

"I ended it." The resulting silence prompted her to glance at her friend, whose expression was inscrutable. "What?"

"Chet was a nice guy."

"Yeah? So?"

"So why did you dump him?"

Why? Why indeed? Other than the fact that she'd woken up one night and stared at him and thought, deep in her panicked soul, *No. No. This is not right.* "He brought his toothbrush over."

Kristi blinked. "Do, ah, you have a toothbrush phobia I don't know about?"

The ferry lunged and Tara grabbed onto the rail to steady herself. "His *toothbrush*, Kristi."

"It's just a toothbrush."

"It's not just a toothbrush." It was a statement. A declaration. It was Chet staking his claim.

"Hmm."

Tara glared at her friend. She knew that *hmm*. "What?"

"Nothing. But… Do you ever wonder…?" It was irritating the way Kristi trailed off. She did that sometimes when she wanted to make a point. Which, when you thought about it, was counterproductive.

"Wonder what?"

"If you might have commitment issues?"

Tara gaped at her. Commitment issues? Hell no.

She didn't *wonder* about that at all.

"It's not an issue." Not for her at least. This wasn't about commitment. It was about survival.

Kristi snorted. "It's your life, Tara. But I never pegged you for someone who wanted to be alone forever."

Why her heart stuttered, why her breath snagged at those words was a mystery. She wasn't afraid of being alone. Hell, she loved being alone. It was her favorite thing in the ever-lovin, frickin world.

"I date."

"I'm not talking about dating. Or casual relationships. I'm talking about something more lasting."

"Like you and Cam?"

Kristi blushed. "Hopefully." Their relationship was new. Brand spanking new. It probably still had all the tags.

That acid reflux thing—the thing that tasted a little like envy—rose again and Tara swallowed it. "I am happy for you, Kristi. I hope this thing with Cam works out—"

"Thank you."

"But I don't think LTRs are for me."

"Because you dump them as soon as they mention toothbrushes." Kristi shot her a crooked grin. "I'm just saying, maybe it's time to think about why you shy away from long-term relationships—"

Tara frowned. She didn't need to think about it. She knew damn well why.

"And ask yourself what you really want out of life. If you really want to be single, then I am right here pulling for you. But if, in your heart of hearts, you're craving a deeper connection… you're doing it wrong."

God bless Kristi. She didn't pull any punches.

She was way off base with this one, but Tara knew her annoying lecture came from the heart.

She forced a smile. "Thank you Kristi."

"I love you Tara," she said with another hug, "I want you to be happy."

Happy. Schmappy.

Her life was fine, wonderful, perfect just the way it was.

They turned back to go inside—because it was truly raining now—and Tara's attention snagged on Devlin Fox, sitting in the cafeteria, with his evil minions, playing cards. She yanked her gaze away.

He was too damn attractive for comfort.

She didn't like the feelings that rose up when she looked at him. Or accidentally caught a glimpse of him out of the corner of her eye. Or thought of him.

So she wouldn't.

And Kristi's advice, bless her meddling little heart, she wouldn't think about that either.

CHAPTER FOUR

Devlin was still obsessing over Ponytail Girl when he arrived home, jogging up the ramp, pushing through the door and tossing his keys into the dish by the door. What she'd done stuck in his craw. That he hadn't been able to seduce her as he planned stuck in his craw as well.

His craw was pretty crowded.

But as much as she aggravated him, she intrigued him more.

Charlie's bag was in the foyer. "Honey, I'm home," he called, stepping over it. He never knew when Charlie would show up, but the bag, dropped wherever it landed, was usually a good clue his on-again off-again housemate had returned.

Charlie was a restless soul, but with good reason.

"In here," a deep voice called.

Devlin made his way into the kitchen and leaned against the jamb, crossing his arms over his chest. Charlie sat at the table surrounded by the remnants of an epic breakfast. The kitchen appeared as though a tornado had blown through. Pancake batter dribbled on the stove, greasy paper towels were balled up by the microwave, milk dripped from the counter onto the floor. Devlin bit his tongue.

He wasn't a clean freak by any stretch of the imagination, but this mess was making his recessive OCD gene itch. He pulled out a chair and plopped down across from his brother and snagged a pancake, focusing on it so he wouldn't have to look at features that were so much like his—but not…anymore. It hurt to look at Charlie now. As though it opened a door, allowing his twin's pain to seep into his soul.

"How was your trip?"

Charlie took a slurp of coffee. "Awesome."

Devlin grunted. Though he made a hell of a mess, Charlie made a hell of a pancake. "Where did you go again?"

"San Fran. Haight Ashbury." Charlie waggled his brows. The movement drew Devlin's attention to the scars on the right side of his face. He quickly glanced away.

"You were…gone a long time." Devlin tried very hard to keep the reproof from his tone. Charlie hated it when he went "all parental." But it was impossible not to worry. His brother would up and disappear, be gone for months and then pop up, grinning like a pup that had found an unattended pan of pot roast.

It would probably be different if Charlie weren't a cripple. He probably wouldn't worry so much then if his brother disappeared for months at a time. Hell, they were both grownups, but he couldn't help worrying. Charlie was his brother. He loved him so much it hurt. And after what he'd been through, he needed someone to take care of him. Worry about him. Protect him.

Charlie had always been the one looking out for Devlin. Now it was his turn to return the favor.

If only he would cooperate.

When his brother had come home, a wounded warrior who had lost the use of his legs in Afghanistan, it had been natural for Devlin to take him in. He'd done a bunch of work making his house wheelchair friendly and made accommodations to the mother-in-law suite on the first floor. He'd been so relieved his brother had survived, he hadn't had much room for any other emotion.

It had been a tough adjustment, bunking with someone just learning to live again. Everything—from how to use the bathroom to how to get into a car—became more complicated when you were in a wheelchair. But they'd done it. Together.

But that challenge was nothing compared to the one Devlin faced now. Charlie's drive for independence. It was as though Charlie was trying to be normal. But he would never be normal again.

The real kicker came when his brother went out and bought a car with hand controls. He came and went as he pleased. At all hours. It was driving Devlin crazy.

Charlie grinned. It was a shit-eating grin. "I met a woman."

"You met a woman? In Haight Ashbury?" Christ. How safe was that? "You used protection, right?"

"For God's sake, Dev, back the fuck off." A thread of exasperation wove through Charlie's tone. "I'm not a baby."

Devlin folded his fingers together and stared at them, unsure how to respond. No, Charlie wasn't a baby, but he didn't seem to realize the gravity of his situation. He would never walk again. He needed to be careful. He shouldn't go gallivanting around the country, picking up stray women in a modern day Sodom and Gomorrah. He should stay at home. Where Devlin knew he was safe.

"You left your bag in the foyer again," he muttered.

Charlie crunched into a piece of toast. Crumbs flaked over his t-shirt. "I'll get it later."

Annoyance bubbled as Devlin skated another glance around the room. His gaze stalled on a pile of eggshells by the fridge; little pools of egg whites slimed the countertop. The little hairs on his neck stood up as the prospect of salmonella rose its ugly head.

"Um… You're going to clean this up, right?" The words came out before he could stop them.

His brother smirked and wheeled over to pour himself another cup of coffee. Devlin grimaced as he missed the cup and a big brown splotch landed on the tile. "You know I'm disabled." He put out a lip in a mocking pout. "I think I'd better leave the cleanup to you."

The dig did not miss its mark. Charlie made no secret of the fact that he resented his brother's overprotective tendencies. A snort made its way out of Devlin's nose.

Wheels squeaked into the uncomfortable silence as Charlie came back to the table. "So…" he said in a too-cheery voice. "How was *your* weekend?" When Devlin didn't respond, his brother gored him with a look. "Didja meet a girl?"

Heat crept up his cheeks as he searched for an answer. If he told his brother the truth about what had happened with Ponytail, he'd never let him live it down. "I met someone."

"Didja get laid?"

The heat expanded. Hot prickles bloomed between his shoulder blades. "Not exactly."

Charlie barked a laugh. "Imagine that. Devlin Fox struck out? Someone call the papers."

"I've struck out before." Not much. But at least one other time he could think of. Usually he had good luck with women. He couldn't fathom what had gone wrong this time.

"It's bound to happen. When you go through women like toilet paper, at some point, you're gonna hit the cardboard."

"I do not go through women like toilet paper." What a crass analogy.

"Okay. Paper towels then. Point is… you're a hound dog."

The dig hit Devlin like a lance. He did date a lot of women and his relationships didn't last very long. But it wasn't that he was licentious or fickle. He'd just never found *her*. That one woman perfect he wanted to spend the rest of his life with. Besides, Charlie had no room to talk.

"That's the pot calling the kettle horny."

"Dude. I'm not the one with blue balls this morning. So, what was her name, this paragon of female fortitude?"

Shit. His brother had a way of homing right in on a wound. "No clue. She told me to call her Sugar."

"Hmm." Charlie stroked his beard, drawing Devlin's attention to the pocked scars on the right side of his face. He forced his gaze elsewhere. "I'm guessing that's not her real name."

"Probably not." The only thing he knew about her was that she was a friend of Lane Daniels'. Trouble was, he and Lane weren't on speaking terms at the moment. Why Lane was pissed at him, he had no clue. He'd only hit on Lucy that one time. On top of that, Lane and Lucy were divorced. Besides, Lucy had shot him down.

"It's probably her stripper name."

Devlin's simmering mortification boiled into fury. Which surprised him. He never lost his temper with Charlie, not since he'd come home in a wheelchair. Despite his brother's attempts to get a rise out of him. He knew nothing about this chick. For all he knew, she *could* be a stripper. Still… "She's not a stripper," he snapped.

"Whoa. Dial it back, bro," Charlie held up a hand. "I was joking. Wow. A snarl and everything…" Ironically, he seemed pleased at the feral reaction.

Devlin raked back his hair and sucked in a breath. "Sorry. I…"

"Dude. No problem." Charlie grinned. "It's nice when you snap. Reminds me of…old times." Yeah, he and his brother had had more than one knock-down drag-out. They'd made sibling rivalry a blood sport. But things were different now. Everything was different now.

"Remember when you didn't treat me with kid gloves?"

Devlin set his teeth to keep back a caustic comment. He knew his brother was baiting him, but he was not inclined to engage. Not like that. Charlie needed to be handled with kid gloves. He deserved it.

So instead he fixed a smile on his face. "Dinner at Beth's tonight. We'll leave at six." Since their parents had died, their sister had taken on hosting the traditional Fox family Sunday night supper.

"Great. I'll drive."

Devlin blanched. Charlie always wanted to drive. And riding in a car with Charlie at the wheel gave him hives. "I'll drive."

"I'm a good driver." Charlie scowled. "I am a very good driver."

"Like *Rainman?*"

The scowl deepened and Devlin winced as he realized the implications of what he'd said. His brother was physically challenged, not mentally challenged. And clearly, Charlie didn't appreciate the unintended association. He spun his wheelchair away from the table and headed for his room. "Whatever. I'm beat. I am going to take a nap. See you later."

The door slammed and Devlin flinched.

Not because his brother had slammed the door, but because he'd escaped. And left a hell of a mess for Devlin to clean up.

And because he knew he'd probably cut Charlie deeply with that flippant comment…when hurting his brother was the last thing he ever wanted to do.

Dinner at Beth's was a trial. Oh, it started out all nice and friendly. These things often did. But Charlie was pissed that Devlin had insisted on driving and missed no opportunity to peck at Devlin's buttons like a chicken with OCD. On crack. Their sister tried to keep the peace, but she should have known better. When Charlie got in that mood, he was unstoppable.

Cal thought their bickering was amusing, but he was seven and easily entertained by puerile pursuits. Beth and Steve merely rolled their eyes and, eventually, talked amongst themselves as though a Battle Royale were not erupting in the midst of their dining room.

Devlin tried to keep his cool, but Charlie knew right where to aim his thrusts and, to his mortification, the meal ended in a blow out. He thought about going home alone and leaving his brother there for

Beth to deal with, but of course he would never do that.

To *her*.

Instead he loaded his brother into his car, and the wheelchair into the trunk and they drove home in a heated silence.

Charlie left the next day. He didn't bother to tell Devlin where he was going or when he would be back.

He tried not to let his frustration, or guilt, overwhelm him. He wanted to help his brother, but he didn't know how.

And Charlie, apparently, didn't want his help to begin with.

To take his mind off all that shit, Devlin went to the island the next weekend, but he ended up going alone. He and Ash had planned to go together, but his buddy had backed out because of a family emergency. He'd tossed Devlin the keys and exhorted him not to throw up on anything.

On their last trip, a drunken Richie had christened every piece of furniture in the living room. Ash and Parker had spent hours cleaning it up. Evidently Ash was still pissed. But Devlin didn't drink like Richie. He barely drank at all. And he'd never barfed on someone else's furniture.

Upon reflection he was glad to be going over alone. Especially glad Richie wasn't coming.

He hadn't gone to the island expecting to see her—really, he hadn't—but when he walked into Darby's Bar and Grill on Friday evening, there she was, leaning over the pool table taking a shot. The vision she made, with her ass all pooched out like that made him drool. The fact that she was alone didn't hurt.

He casually strolled through the near-empty bar into the pool hall in the back and leaned against her table watching as she sighted her shot. She peeped up at him as she took it. The cue ball went askew. It was tough holding back his smirk at her horrified expression.

So he didn't.

"Fancy meeting you here," he murmured.

She ignored him and came around the table to take another shot. She missed that one too. Judging from the frown she sent him, she considered it his fault. He should have walked away. Gone to the bar and ordered a keg of beer or something, but he didn't. He watched her play. Because it annoyed her. And she was damn sexy when she was annoyed. That was enough motivation for any man.

The waitress who had saved his ass the week before made her way over. When she recognized him, she grinned. She flicked a telling glance down at his jeans. "Can I, um, get you anything?" she asked on a chuckle.

"Just a beer, please."

She nodded. "Any particular brand?"

"You choose." All Darby's stock was excellent. Devlin had no doubt he'd be getting the most expensive brew on tap.

"And for you?" The waitress turned to his nemesis. "Want another?"

Ponytail upended her glass, a tumbler, and then nodded. "Yes please. Gin. Straight with lime."

The waitress picked up her glass and headed back to the bar.

"Gin? Straight with lime?" No wonder she was missing shots.

"It's been a long week." This, she muttered.

"Well. It is Friday."

"So it is."

"And here we are."

"Here we are." She took another shot and landed the ball in the side pocket with a sharp crack. Too bad it was the eight ball. She grumbled to herself and racked up the balls.

"I'm Devlin," he said, thrusting out his hand, reminding her. In case she'd forgotten.

She ignored it. "I know."

Youch.

"And you are…"

The look she sent him could freeze water. "Not. Interested."

Yeah. Right. He remembered the hunger on her face when she'd had a hold of his cock. She was interested.

At least, he hoped she was.

He was.

Was he ever.

A weekend fling? With an opportunity to exact some sweet revenge? In bed? *Why yes, thank you.*

All he had to do was convince *her.*

He picked up a cue. "I'll play you."

She sniffed. "I'd rather play alone."

"Shame for you to have to play with yourself." He probably shouldn't have infused the *double entendre* with such a smarmy tone, but he liked the way it made her nostrils flare.

"Go over there." She waved at one of the other empty tables.

"I'd rather play with you." He cleared his throat. "We never finished our game last weekend…"

The color rising on her cheeks was delightful. She turned away. "Okay. That was a shitty thing to do," she said softly. So softly, he nearly didn't make it out.

"'Scuse me?"

"I said sorry. Okay?" Yeah. He heard that. Because she bellowed it. So loudly, it appeared to surprise even her. "I was really pissed at you."

He clutched his chest. "At me?"

"And when I'm pissed, I like to get even." She was a beautiful woman. Her face was perfection, but the way she narrowed her eyes and hissed through her teeth gave him pause. Damn. Not a woman to piss off.

"What the hell did I do to you?" They'd never even met…

Her eyes narrowed even more, into little slits, like an angry kitten about to swipe off an offending hand. "You don't even know?"

Devlin gaped at her. His mind whirled. "No. I don't."

She leaned against her cue and glowered at him. In that pose, she looked like an ancient warrior prepared for battle. "I own a bakery."

"And?"

She leaned in. "You reviewed my bakery."

Shit.

"I…ah. What's the name of your bakery?"

"Stud. Muffin." The way she said it made it clear she expected him not to remember. But he did. That was an awesome bakery. One of his favorites, though he rarely got to that end of town.

Now that he knew where she worked, he'd have to make the trek more often.

"That was not a bad review."

"Three burps." Damn. The girl could growl. "You gave it three fucking burps."

"Three burps is a good review." It was a damn good review. Most eateries would breathe a sigh of relief to get two burps from him.

She tossed her cue onto the table. "Three burps sucks. Plus, you had the audacity to complain that I don't have gluten-free."

He leaned forward. "Do you?"

If she narrowed her eyes any more, she'd be blind. "That is not the point."

"That's exactly the point. If you don't have gluten-free, then you don't have gluten-free. There's a large population of people in Seattle who don't eat wheat and they need to know if—"

"It's a bakery! I use flour. So frickin sue me!"

They glared at each other across the table. Well, she glared. He stared. Because in a flurry of passion, she was pretty damn intriguing. Her color was high, her lips parted, a fierceness etched her features.

He wanted to kiss her.

He wanted to kiss her bad.

Charmaine arrived just then with their drinks. Devlin pulled out a couple twenties and handed them to her. "Keep the change."

"Thanks." She slipped the bills into her pocket with a wink. "Give me a wave if you want another."

"Sure thing." Devlin watched her walk away, barely focusing on the twitch of her ass. When he turned back to his companion, he winced at her expression.

"I can buy my own drinks," his pretty baker snapped.

"Take the damn drink. It's not a marriage proposal, for God's sake." Devlin smiled. An attempt to placate her, which didn't work. "Consider it an apology. An extra burp, if you will."

"Fine," she grunted. "One drink. Then we're even." She took a snort of her drink and unracked the balls, taking the first shot without flipping for it. But Devlin didn't care, because when he stepped in to take the second shot, she let him.

And she was drinking her drink. So they were even. Excellent.

"But it hardly counts as an extra burp," she muttered.

He blew out a breath. "I'm telling you, three burps is a damn good review. You should see the review I gave Billy Bob's Burger and Beer."

"I *love* Billy Bob's."

"Those onion rings could give Dracula a heart attack."

"Those onion rings are heaven on earth."

"Greasy as hell. I could see through my napkin when I blotted them."

She studied him for a moment, then snorted, "Baby."

Something about her demeanor tickled him. Or maybe it was the fact that he was finally—*finally*—having a conversation with her. Or that he'd figured out why she was so mad at him—and what a relief that was. Regardless, something in her demeanor tickled him and he busted out laughing.

She propped her fists on her hips and frowned at him, but he could see the amusement in her eyes. And then her lips twitched. And then she chuckled.

And he knew he had her.

He knew he would have her.

Sometime this weekend he would have this woman in his bed.

But first, he needed to discover her name.

CHAPTER FIVE

Tara stared at Devlin as he leaned over the table to take a shot.

Damn.

She'd been attracted to him the minute she laid eyes on him. When she'd plowed into him on the ferry, sealed against him from chest to groin, when his large hands had gripped her hips to keep her from plunging down the stairs, the heat between then had been undeniable.

But when she'd discovered his nefarious identity, an unquenchable fury had consumed her. The desire to make him pay.

That, combined with a couple of drinks, had resulted in her hair-brained idea to seduce him and leave him hanging…so to speak.

She'd never expected the regret that had haunted her for the past week. She'd relived every moment of their aborted tryst over and over again. And in most of her fantasies…she hadn't walked away. In many of them, they'd ended up wound together in a steamy tangle of limbs.

He took his shot and stood, flicking a surreptitious glance at her. It was quick. It was scorching. Excitement fluttered in her belly.

Damn.

He was, without exception, the most attractive man she'd ever met.

And on top of it all, he had to go and be charming.

No one had ever charmed her out of a snit so easily.

She kind of resented the fact that he could. He could smile and make a quip about burps and buy her a drink and all of a sudden, her resentment washed away in a tsunami of lust.

And this was lust. Wasn't it?

She took her last shot, winning the game.

He put out a lip in an alluring pout, though she suspected he'd let her win. "Want to play again?" Without waiting for her response, he racked the balls. He did, however, wait for her nod before he positioned himself for the break.

But then he paused. "We should...play for something."

His tone irritated her. Or maybe it wasn't irritation. The glint in his eye was scintillating.

She leaned on her cue. "Like what?"

He stood, looming over her, forcing her to tip her head to see his face. Well, the underside of his chin at least. God, it was gorgeous. A gorgeous chin. "How about...a dare?"

That shimmy again. A cold-hot ripple through her womb. "A-a dare?" She forced herself to appear blasé, though she felt anything but.

"Sure." He bent closer. So close she could taste the earthy beer on his breath. "You seem like a daring sort. Besides...I owe you." A whisper. Then he grinned. It was a wicked offering that made dread crawl up her spine. Or maybe not dread...

Whatever. The heat made her uncomfortable, so she snorted. Glanced away.

It was as though he knew her. Knew she couldn't resist a dare. She never could. She fiddled with her cue. His eyes tracked the motion. His tongue peeped out to wet his lower lip. As though he was thinking about tasting...something.

"Okay," she said at long last. "What kind of dare?"

He cleared his throat. "If I win..." His lips curled up at that. "You tell me your name."

Tara blinked. That was not the dare she'd been expecting. She'd been expecting him to ask her to finish what she'd started the last time they tangled. Anticipating that, perhaps. "My name?"

"The whole name and nothing but the name."

"And if I win?"

He shrugged. "Whatever you want."

She studied him for a moment running scenarios in her head. Oh, there were a couple things that leapt to mind. Crowded her mind, in fact. She pressed them away. She was still infuriated with him over that piss poor review. He should suffer a little bit; a mere fraction of the mortification she'd felt when she'd read that blog. What would mortify a big, manly man like Devlin Fox? Ah, yes.

"The Macarena."

He blinked. "The…Macarena?"

"Yup. Here. Now. In this bar. You do the Macarena." She leaned in and hissed, "With no music."

His chin firmed with what she imagined was determined resolve. He moved closer until they were nearly nose-to-nose, until she could see the sea-foam flecks in his irises. "I can handle that."

"Fine."

"Fine."

"Good."

"Good."

She nodded. "Let's play."

"Let's do this thing." He bent over the table and took his shot. The crack of the break echoed in the room. Three striped balls rolled into pockets as though he were the puppet master and they were on strings.

Tara frowned, suspecting he'd been sandbagging her in the last game. When he missed the next shot, she stepped up to the table. Concentrating hard, she took her shot. She sank the seven, five and three in succession, but the one banked of the edge of the corner pocket. *Damn.*

He aimed for the eleven and sank it. Then the fifteen. And the nine. He had one ball left, not counting the eight ball. Sweat beaded her brow. She wiped her palms on her jeans. She didn't know why she was so nervous. They were only playing for a name. Her name. But she desperately wanted to see him dance the Macarena. She desperately wanted to beat him.

When he missed on the twelve, her breath came out in a whoosh. Marshalling her reserves, she focused and dropped the four, two and six. Then the one. She rounded the table heading for the eight, her final ball. With flawless form, she nailed it.

The crow of victory was probably not necessary, but it felt damn good.

She turned to him with a smirk. Drew a saucy circle with her finger. "Dance."

A blush crept up his cheeks. He laid his cue on the table and launched into a credible version of the Macarena—one arm out, then the other, palms upturned—then to the hips. All the while, whispering the words to himself.

Her response was a barked laugh, a trill of exhilaration—because he was doing it. And damn, was he cute. But when he got to the hip wiggle, her laugh petered out as another emotion engulfed her. Another vision—a fantasy—filled her muddled mind. A vision that had been hovering there, lingering in her imagination, for a week.

Devlin Fox was a hot guy—she knew that—but she hadn't realized how deeply she wanted him, had no clue that a little swizzle of his hips would hit her so hard. Like a freaking Mack truck of hunger.

By the time he finished she was drooling.

It was probably the gin coursing in her veins—but she doubted it. This felt more like lust. Pure and unadulterated.

It annoyed the crap out of her.

Humiliating him hadn't quite worked out the way she'd intended.

"Well?" He put his hands on his hips and gazed at her.

She swallowed heavily…so she could speak without a spray. "Fine. That was fine."

He grinned. "Another game?"

A hint of panic snarled in her belly. "I, ah, have to get back." Yeah. The last thing she wanted was to play another game with him, and perhaps lose.

"Chicken?"

Her heart stuttered. *Shit.* He could read her like a book. "I'm not chicken. I just have to get back." She glanced at her watch, though she wasn't wearing one. "My friends are waiting." A lie. She'd come this weekend with Kristi, who was probably in the middle of a hot clinch with Cam right now. Bella and Holt had come too. They were probably clinching as well. Everyone was clinching. Except Tara. She tried not to let that annoy her too.

It was her choice to be single right now. She needed to focus on her business.

Men just got in the way.

Oh sure, it started off all fuckity-fun, but then, inevitably, the guy would get all demanding and overbearing. Possessive. Toothbrushes everywhere…

And that was when her warning system would kick into gear. That was when the little voice in the back of her head would start whispering, "No. He's not the one." Not the one who could give her that elusive security, that *forever* she craved.

But forever was probably a fantasy anyway.

Chet had been particularly annoying in the end. While she had enjoyed the companionship—and God knew she liked her sex—it wasn't worth the hassle to put up with his crap. Not when she knew their relationship wasn't *going* anywhere. Besides, when a girl needed to be in bed by seven in the pm—and up at three—there was a very short window for kinky fuckery.

So she'd broken it off with Chet a month ago and she hadn't been laid since.

Her libido was not appreciative. Some days she wore lust like a cloak. She thought about sex all the time—and more so since she'd done that little dance with Devlin on the ferry.

She didn't relish the thought of lying in her cold and lonely bed all weekend listening to muffled moans from the rooms on either side of her.

And now she had that vision of Devlin swizzling his hips to contend with. His muscles bunching beneath the fabric of his t-shirt as he danced the Macarena for her pleasure. The pink peep of his tongue as he concentrated on the moves.

He leaned against the table with a snort. She tried not to fixate on his long, lean denim-clad legs. "It's Friday night. Are you really going back at eight?"

Was it only eight? It felt like midnight. "It's past my bedtime." A smirk.

"Come on, Ponytail. One more game."

"What did you call me?"

He reached around and yanked on her hair. "Ponytail." He shrugged. "What else should I call you? Beautiful?"

She glared at him. Not because he thought she was beautiful, but because he was clearly teasing.

"Gluten girl?" He winked. "Sugar Muffin?"

She crossed her arms. "Ponytail is fine."

He gave a mock bow. "Ponytail it is."

Damn it, he was exasperating.

And adorable.

She bit her lip to keep a smile from slipping out. He would see a smile as some bizarre form of encouragement. She was certain of it.

As though she had acquiesced to another game, he collected the balls and racked them. "What shall we play for this time?" His steamy expression made it clear he would be asking for something far more daring than a name.

Temptation prodded her. She knew it was stupid to tangle with a guy like this. He was far too attractive for his own good. And she was so frickin horny she could taste it.

But so what? So what if she lost a game and had to give him her name, or a kiss or…

She stiffened her spine. "What did you have in mind?"

He studied her, stroking his pool cue as he considered his options, then winced as he followed her gaze and realized how suggestive the movement was. He blushed and chalked his cue.

His blush deepened when he realized the scrape of the chalk over the tender tip of his cue was far more lurid.

His chagrin amused her. And she liked that he wasn't a cold-hearted predator, hunting females. Or a smarmy come-on artist. That some modicum of chivalry nested in his soul. At least enough for him to blush.

Would it be so terrible to use him to slake her hunger?

Just once?

Nothing more than that, certainly.

And he did *owe* her. At least one more burp.

"Do you…" He cleared his throat. "Do you like peanut butter?"

She gaped at him. "Peanut butter?"

"Some people are allergic."

"I'm not allergic. You want me to make you a sandwich?"

He fixed his scorching attention on her. It burned. "No. Loser has to lick peanut butter from some portion of the winner's body."

The way he said it, whispered it, sent a jolt of electricity sizzling along her nerves. A vision of finishing what she had started in the alley last week skewered her like a bolt. Not that she'd thought about it, imagined it. Much.

Tension between them ratcheted up. The bubble of attraction surrounding them tightened.

"That, um, that sounds pretty intimate." Not that she minded. But it was quite a leap from 'tell me your name.'

His attention shifted to her breasts, then trickled down and down, lingering here or then and landing on her feet. Her toes curled at the heat in his stare. He cleared his throat again. "I...really like peanut butter."

"I...we don't have any peanut butter."

"I have some. At my place."

"Ah...and your...roommates?"

He scratched at his neck. Ran a finger around the collar of his t-shirt. "I'm here alone."

Holy hell.

They were close. Face to face. Almost nose to nose. He smelled delicious. Heat wafted off him in waves. She remembered what it felt like, that second of bliss, when they'd been chest to chest on the ferry. And she ached.

One night. One fling. Just one.

"Okay."

Shock flickered over his features, but only for a moment. Then he regained control of himself and gulped. "Okay?"

She nodded. Grinned. Elation swamped her, body and soul. Because she'd made a decision. When Tara Romano made a decision, she was all in.

And because she really did love peanut butter.

CHAPTER SIX

She'd said yes.

He could hardly believe it.

It didn't matter if he won or lost the stupid game. Someone was licking someone tonight. And he doubted it would stop there.

Of course, there was always the possibility she was playing him, as she did last week. There was always the possibility she would lather his cock up with creamy peanut butter—it would be creamy, wouldn't it? Crunchy might be a little too kinky for his tastes—and then laugh and walk away.

That would be a hell of a mess to clean up.

But what the heck. A guy had to take a risk once in a while. Especially if the potential prize was a woman like this on her knees, lapping at his…

Shit.

He focused on calming his raging hard on. He could barely bend over the table to shoot. Not that it mattered. Win or lose, he won. The thought of licking peanut butter from between her delicate toes was nearly as alluring. She would probably choose the foot. Judging from what he knew of her, she would revel in having him kiss her feet. He would revel in that as well. God. What he wouldn't give to watch her squirm…

"Darlings!"

It took a moment for Devlin to emerge from the fantasy he'd been weaving in his head to realize the high-pitched call was directed at them.

A beautiful nymph with long flowing blonde hair tripped in six-inch heels through the pistachio shells scattered on the floor—heading straight for them. *Crap.* Devlin tried not to grimace.

She stopped, repositioning her Gucci purse beneath her arm. "I didn't know you two were here this weekend." Her gaze skated from Ponytail to Devlin and back again. "And I didn't know you knew each other." Her lashes batted. They were long and lush and probably horribly expensive. Everything Avery Warner did was expensive and over the top. She wiggled her lacquered nails in their direction. Her diamonds flashed, even in the dim light. "Are you two…a thing?"

"No," Ponytail snapped, a little too quickly.

They exchanged a glance. She responded to his frown with one of her own. "No." Devlin repeated. "We just—"

But as usual, Avery didn't let him finish. Avery rarely let anyone finish. "Well, you look good together."

"We are not together," his companion bleated. She shouldn't have. The heat in her tone captured Avery's attention. Captured it so much, she narrowed her eyes and scrutinized them both.

It was uncomfortable being analyzed by Avery Warner. Something like that never ended well. Avery excelled at mischief. And it was usually always a little twisted.

She smiled. Like a reptile. If reptiles had glossy, pink lips. "Well," she gushed. "You must come to my birthday party tomorrow. You simply must." She leaned in and winked. "It's a BDSM themed party."

Devlin swallowed heavily. He'd been to one of Avery's parties before. He'd barely escaped with his manhood intact. "Tomorrow? Gee, I…"

"I'd love to come," Ponytail said with a glint in her eye. It was a glint that surprised Devlin. He hadn't pegged her for a kinky girl. But he liked that she was open to…options.

"Wonderful." Avery pinned Ponytail with a gimlet glance. "And are any of the other Dawgs here?"

"Holt and Bella—"

A low, evil chuckle. "Oh, they *have* to come."

"And Kristi and Cam."

Avery wrinkled her nose. "You can invite them, but Kristi is pretty *vanilla.*"

Ponytail grinned. "Drew is supposed to come this weekend, as well as Lane. But I don't know when they're getting here."

Devlin stiffened. Lane was coming? *Great.* The last time he'd seen Lane Daniels, the bastard had threatened to flatten his nose. For a divorced guy, Lane was pretty territorial about his ex.

That sealed it. He was definitely not going to the party.

"Well, invite them all. The party's at my place tomorrow and starts at nine on the dot. Don't be late," Avery said with a smirk. "There are forfeits for latecomers." She chuckled at her own joke. Avery always appreciated a pithy *double entendre.* Even when no one else got it. "And you!" She spun on Devlin, pointing an exquisitely manicured finger in his direction. "You'd better be there. With fucking bells on."

"Yes ma'am. Jingle, jingle." He tendered a little salute. He had no intention of going, of course. If things went his way tonight, he and Ponytail would be deep in a playtime of their own. Far too busy to go to the big house on the bluff and prance around in leather, sucking on penis-pops and avoiding the outrageous games Avery liked to play. Games where one never knew who might end up wearing handcuffs and a dog collar.

And if it was Avery's birthday party, there would, no doubt, be spankings. Probably a lot of them. While Devlin didn't mind the prospect of bringing his hand down on Ponytail's shapely ass, he knew, if roles were reversed, she'd be ruthless.

Yeah. Party or not, his plan was to seduce her tonight and keep her in his bed all weekend. The party would have to go on without them.

Avery didn't stay long after exacting the promises she required. She flounced to the bar to flirt with Darby. Devlin knew she was flirting, and mercilessly so, on account of his blush—visible even from here. Darby, who owned and ran the only bar on the island, was painfully shy and never dated, as far as Devlin could tell.

It seemed as though Avery wanted to eat him alive. She probably did.

"Shall we continue our…game?" Ponytail's low sultry tones recaptured his attention and he turned back to the table. Her expression pole axed him. "We were playing for peanut butter, I believe."

"Yes. We were." He swallowed. "I, ah, where were we?"

"It was my shot." The way she tried to hide her impish grin told him it was not her shot, but he let it go. He hardly cared who won.

He waved at the table. "Be my guest."

She flicked him a thoughtful glance before bending to sight along the cue.

Devlin stepped back. And enjoyed the view.

Yeah, he wouldn't mind draping her over his lap and having those lush globes splayed before him. Preferably bare, but he would work with whatever he got. His fingers curled at the thought of how nice his handprint would look on those rounded globes.

A minx like this deserved a spanking. Especially after the way she'd teased him. Was still teasing him.

As though she could read his thoughts, she gave her ass a little waggle as she prepared to shoot.

Damn.

Damn, damn.

Maybe he did want to win. The thought of her ass covered with peanut butter made his knees weak. But if he won, there was no doubt in his mind exactly where that peanut butter would go. She'd be finishing what she started last week. He quickly reviewed the contents of Ash's pantry, wondering how much peanut butter there was.

She sank the first ball but missed on the second. "Your turn," she grunted.

"Yeah." He stepped up to the table and surveyed the layout of the balls. There were a couple cheap shots—he took them—and then one that was a little more challenging. A trill of excitement slashed him as the ball banked off the felt and landed in the pocket with a neat click. One more to go.

He bent and sighted the ball, and drew back the cue.

Just as he was about to shoot, she cleared her throat. "Is it me, or is it warm in here?"

His gaze snapped to her. Not only because her tone was low and sultry. But because a flutter of movement in the vicinity of her breasts—which were always somewhere on his radar—indicated she was unbuttoning her blouse.

And hell. She was.

One. Two. Three buttons. Until the cleft of her cleavage was clearly visible. She fanned herself there, much lower than was precisely necessary, and then drew her fingertips slowly along that shadowy crease.

Devlin's muscles locked. His pulse set up a manic tattoo that resonated throughout his body—pounded in his cock.

Shit.

He affected a nonchalant mien. Clucked his tongue. "Cheaters never prosper, Ponytail."

"I'm not cheating."

"Aren't you?"

"I'm simply making an observation. It is warm in here. Isn't?"

Hell yeah it was.

"You know…I think I'd like peanut butter here," she murmured in a pouty voice, tracing her cleavage again. She leaned closer. Touched a nipple, clearly outlined against the fabric of her blouse. "Or here. What do you think, Devlin?"

Think? There was no thinking.

Without glancing at the table, he took his shot. Satisfaction flared as he heard the telltale thunk as the eight ball found its home.

"I win." He hardly needed to say it. Judging from her grunt of dismay, she knew damn well her ploy hadn't worked. But it felt good to say.

It also felt good to take her hand and lead her from the bar.

And even better when she followed without demur.

Ash's house wasn't far from town, but on this night, the trek felt like a million miles. They did not speak as they made their way along the beach path. The moon was out and the sky was clear. A thousand pinprick stars glittered in the heavens. A gentle breeze carried the briny scent of the ocean inland. Waves shushed in the distance.

And her hand. Her hand was warm in his.

He loved that, as they walked—with a little more purpose than one might normally stroll home after an evening at the bar—her fingers wove through his.

He paused at the stairs leading up the hill to Ash's house. Tipped up her chin with two fingers. "Are you sure about this?" he asked.

She narrowed her eyes and puckered her brows. "A bet's a bet."

Yeah. It was. Still… "A game is a game too. And I'll be frank Ponytail…" She opened her mouth to respond but he silenced her with a finger. "I want you. I want you pretty fuckin' bad. But not because I won a bet."

This seemed to surprise her. Her lips worked. "But… You did win."

"I know. But despite what you may think of me, I'm not the kind of guy to take advantage of a woman simply because she can't resist a dare—"

"That is—"

"If you come inside, it's because you want to come inside. Because you feel it too. This draw between us. Understood?"

Where this chivalry came from, he had no clue. Then again, maybe it wasn't chivalry at all. Maybe it was a deep scorching need to know. Know that she wanted him with the same aching desperation.

She studied him for a moment, the moonlight kissing her face, imbuing her with an ethereal glow. Her eyes were magnificent. Wide. Clear. Her mouth ripe and full. He ached to kiss her, but he did not. Could not. Not until he knew.

"Are you releasing me from the bet?" She spoke so softly he almost didn't hear her.

He nodded. "If you want to be released."

It seemed to befuddle her, this concept that the choice was hers—to come in or leave. That or the fact that the choice came with a declaration. She had to admit she wanted him. Agree that whatever happened with him was her choice, and not a result of the obligation of some stupid dare.

This took her a moment—an eternity—to process. His heart thudded into the silence. Then she tipped her chin and nodded. "Yes."

He cupped her cheeks and tipped her chin so he could see her. "What? I didn't hear you."

"Yes." He stared at her lips as they moved. Fascinated by them. Beguiled by the scent of her. The feathery tease of her breath. "Yes. I want to come in."

The words barely escaped before he sealed her mouth with his. And holy God, what heaven it was. She was soft, submissive, open to him, and so warm. She tasted like ambrosia, a sweet mixture of arousal and surprise.

When she opened to him, welcomed his tongue in its tentative foray, his knees locked. He turned his head and deepened the kiss, pulling her closer, sealing them together. Pleasure skittered through him. She was curvy, pillowy and firm in all the right places. They fit together like puzzle pieces long lost.

She arched into him, wiggling against his cock. Agony speared him. When she tunneled her fingers into his hair and scored him with her nails, he nearly wept.

"God," he groaned. "God." It was all he could think to say. It was all he could manage.

She pulled back first, but it was to whisper, "We should go inside."

She was in the shadows then, her expression hard to read. But he fancied he didn't need to. Her intention was clear. And her hand was on his ass.

He led the way up the stairs and fumbled with the keys for a bit before he finally got the slender metal shard to fit in the infinitesimally small slot. His mind was a little muddled by thoughts of an entry of another kind.

The door opened and they spilled inside. He meant to reach for the light switch, but completely forgot about that when she stepped into his arms and pulled him into another scorching exchange.

Tongues. Lips. Nibbles. Nips. They consumed each other. Madly, hotly, a rampage of need. He backed her up against the wall and kicked the door shut, then found the hem of her blouse and skated his hand beneath it.

Ah.

Her skin was warm. Velvety smooth. He eased higher and higher until he found and cupped her full breast. Snarls of delight and anticipation danced along his spine, nesting in his balls at the weight, the give, of this treasure. Had he ever felt anything more perfect?

Unable to resist, he cupped the other breast, though her shirt. He pressed them together and dipped his head to explore the cleft between them with his tongue, as he had been aching to do since she'd traced it in the bar. He buried his face in her softness and drew in her scent.

Ah. She was fragrant. Some light perfume, or powder or maybe just her.

He found a nipple, a pouty protuberance, and scored it with a nail. She shuddered and released a guttural groan. "Oh, God!"

She took his head in her hands, turned it to the side and nested in his neck, licking and laving and nuzzling the sensitive skin there until he thought he might expire. Unable to move away from such bliss, he held still, held his breath and simply savored the sensations she drew on him with her tongue.

When she nibbled his earlobe, dabbed into the shell of his ear, he nearly lost his load. His overwhelming response to something so simple and small was astounding. But her touch was potent. It took everything in him to hold back the prickles of need goading him, lancing him. He wanted to come, but he needed more.

He reached down and yanked up her leg, wrapping it around his waist. She scrabbled for purchase, but he balanced her, pinned her against the wall, pressing his aching cock against her groin. And rubbed.

She threw back her head and met his gaze.

What he saw there scored him to the core.

Need.

Hunger.

Desire.

"I want you," he grunted. "I want you now."

"Yes," A whisper. But threaded through it, a passion that was not tentative in the slightest.

He flicked open the snap of her jeans. Released her leg and yanked them down, along with her panties. She kicked them off and reached for his zipper.

In her frenzy, her hand brushed against his cock and Devlin closed his eyes. Fought back a whimper.

When she followed his jeans down and knelt before him, his vision went red. She hooked her fingers in the elastic of his briefs and slowly eased them down. His cock, rampant and ready, stood proud.

She released a ragged moan and cupped him, took him in her fist and tested his girth.

Good. So good.

He'd wanted her on her knees before him. Dreamed of it for the past seven nights. Wanted her on her knees before him with his cock buried deep in her throat. But now...

But now, all he could think of was owning her. Possessing her. Planting himself so deeply into her he might never find his way out again. He wouldn't want to.

Gently, he took her shoulders and brought her to her feet. He answered the question in her eyes with a kiss. A ravenous kiss.

Passion rode him. Need and hunger crawled in his belly.

Her moans inflamed him.

Without thought, without premeditation or sanity or finesse, he ripped open her blouse and yanked down the cups of her bra. Though it was dark and they tangled in the shadows, barely in the foyer of the house, the moonlight filtering through the window gleamed off the creamy globes of her breasts. They bobbled as he lifted her up, pinned her against the wall. As though she knew what he needed, as though she needed it desperately too, she wrapped her legs around his waist and tipped her hips. He captured a rosy peak in his mouth and sucked as he slipped inside. Slipped into heaven.

God, she was hot. Hot and tight and slick. He moaned as he sank deeper and deeper still. The tiny muscles of her channel quivered around his invading cock, sending pings of pleasure, shards of exquisite torment, over every nerve, invigorating him. He sucked on her nipple again and felt the reverberation of her groan to the base of his balls.

He shifted her higher, repositioning her against the wall. And began a slow, decadent rhythm. At the end of each thrust he twitched his hips to the side, exploring her depths until he found it.

And oh. He knew when he found it.

She shivered and quailed. She buried her nails in his back and scored him through his t-shirt. She clenched him tight and hissed a sigh.

"Is that it?" he huffed. "Is that what you like?"

"Yes," she growled. The growl became a wail as he withdrew and drove home again. And again. And again.

His pace increased, though there was no intent, no thought behind it. Simply instinct fed by need, hunger, a desperate ache to feel her come around him. To make her loose every scrap of control. To make her wild.

Make her his.

He pounded, hell for leather. Whipping in and out of her. Relishing the illicit slap of skin against wet skin. And she drenched him. As her arousal rose, her body released, easing the friction, allowing for a riotous ride.

He knew when she came. Heard it, felt it, wore it. Her cunt devolved from a tight measured hold to a series of savage spasms, clenching, clasping and then finally clamping down in a manic grip he could not escape. Then again, he didn't want to.

His cock swelled. Cum burned at the base of his balls. He dipped his head and suckled her nipples, dug his fingers deep into the flesh of her ass.

Sanity flew in the force of his orgasm. Like a flood of lava, hot and scorching and delirious to be free, he erupted, filling her.

Even when it was over, he couldn't stop moving, though his thrusts were slow, sleepy, reluctant for it to end.

She was slow to recover too. He held her there, against the wall, buried in her warmth until she caught her breath. She looked up at him and hitched a small laugh.

"What?" he murmured through a kiss.

"We forgot…" she said.

"We forgot what?" His brain was barely functioning, but he was sure they'd left out a lot of things…

"We forgot the peanut butter."

She said this with such a pout, he couldn't help but throw his head back and laugh.

Because there would be time for that…later. They had all night. All weekend. Maybe longer…

Afterwards they curled up together on the sofa to recuperate. He must have dozed off because when he awoke, she was gone. Even though that pissed him off, he found himself laughing.

Because, again, she'd taken his jeans.

His humor didn't stall until he remembered…he still didn't know her name.

CHAPTER SEVEN

Tara nibbled at a smile as she slipped in the back door of the house she shared with her friends, clutching a pair of rumpled jeans to her chest. They smelled of him. Fresh, clean and manly.

She was well on her way to amassing quite a collection.

Sex with Devlin had been amazing. More amazing than she could ever have imagined.

The memory of his cock sliding in and out of her, even now, made her tingle.

She'd awoken from her nap, curled against his hard, warm body on the couch, steeping in the euphoria still bubbling in her womb...until mortification had set in.

Not that she'd fucked him. Hell no. That was an experience she'd clutch to her heart for many long, lonely nights to come. He'd been magnificent. Feral in his passion.

But she hadn't intended to tumble so easily. She'd planned to give him what he wanted...a peanut butter blow job. Planned to bring him to the very edge of insanity, licking and lapping and exploring his thick cock...and then sashay away.

It hadn't worked out that way.

He'd backed her up against the wall and touched her. Kissed her. Fed on her until she was in such a frenzy, she completely forgot about her evil plans. She'd wanted nothing—nothing—but the long slow slide of his cock inside her.

Everything else had been stripped from her brain, as though he'd peeled her civility away and tossed it aside like long-forgotten panties, reduced her to her most primal core.

They hadn't even used a condom.

She was not pleased that he'd forgotten to use a condom.

She was not pleased that she'd forgotten to insist. She always insisted. Even though she was on the pill.

She'd never forgotten. Never been so swept away by passion, by sheer animal lust, that she'd neglected to politely ask a man to wear a raincoat. She lived in Seattle, for God's sake.

That in itself should be enough to remind her how treacherous her feelings for him were.

But it had been phenomenal.

Almost too phenomenal to bear.

Certainly too phenomenal to stomach the awkward *after*.

So she'd slipped away. Like a thief in the night, skulking through the shadows back to the safety of her den.

The lights were on in the great room and she could hear murmured conversation rumbling in the room. She closed the door quietly, tiptoed down the hall and peered into the kitchen, dreading what she might be interrupting.

Anymore, when one was bunking with Kristi and Cam or Bella and Holt, one never knew what kind of shenanigans one might walk in on.

Earlier, she'd blithely tripped downstairs into the rumpus room and discovered Bella and Holt in a…compromising position. Well, Bella was in a compromising position. Tied hand and foot. Getting spanked.

Holt hadn't been compromised at all.

He'd been so into it, he hadn't even noticed the interloper.

Tara had turned tail and sprinted back up the stairs.

Honestly. Would it be too much to ask for them to hang a necktie on the doorknob? Or, in this case, a leash?

But there were no naughty reindeer games happening now. At least, not of the sexual variety. She was relieved to see Cam and Holt, along with Drew at the table playing cards. Probably poker, if she knew them. And she did.

She dumped the purloined jeans on the kitchen counter and pulled out a glass, availing herself of the open bottle of Bombay on the counter. "Hey guys."

"Hey Tara." Drew grinned.

"Where've you been?" Cam asked, tossing out a card.

She tipped up the bottle, sloshing in several fingers of gin. She needed it. "I went to Darby's."

Holt pointedly checked his watch and arched a brow. He didn't need to say a word. She'd been gone far too long for a quick drink at the bar.

She decided to forestall his question with one of her own. "Where are Bella and Kristi?"

"Bella's...taking a nap." Holt's lips quirked. Judging from his expression, Tara didn't want to ask. She didn't need to ask. Poor Bella. Whatever it was, it wasn't a nap.

"Kristi's in the hot tub." Cam thrust his thumb toward the deck.

Tara sliced a lime and squeezed a wedge into her drink. "And you're not with her?"

Cam shrugged. "We don't have to be together every minute of the day." Snorts rounded the room. The two were inseparable lately. "Besides, she likes to stay in there until she prunes." He shifted in his seat. "And I don't want to cook the boys."

Tara chuckled and began rooting around in the fridge. "Anything to eat?" She'd planned to grab a sandwich at Darby's and gotten...distracted. Now she was starving.

"Didn't you eat at the bar?" God damn Holt and his too-sharp eyes.

Tara pulled out a loaf of bread and made a quick turkey sandwich. She would have preferred peanut butter...but she wouldn't think about that. "Hmm. I ran into Avery."

"Avery Warner?" Drew perked up.

"Mmm hmm." She took a bite of her sandwich. "Did you know it's her birthday this weekend?"

"Really?" Holt stood with a scrape of his chair and meandered to the fridge to grab another beer. His gaze stalled on the jeans on the counter and then flicked to her blouse, which she'd tied around her breasts leaving her midriff bare—the way they'd done when they were girls and wanted to pick up guys. She hadn't wanted to pick up guys. But she'd had to do something creative...as Devlin had popped off nearly all the buttons.

Holt said nothing, but the way he cleared his throat was telling.

Tara shot him a mischievous smirk. "You're all invited to the party tomorrow."

Holt twisted the lid off his beer and tossed it into the trash. "But I didn't bring a gift."

"You know Avery. She'd consider your luminous presence at her BDSM party as a gift in itself."

"Christ." Drew buried his face in his hands. "It's a BDSM party?"

"You expected Hello Kitty?" Cam chuckled, popping a handful of cashews into his mouth.

"Only if Hello Kitty was sporting a cat-o-nine." Sometimes Holt had a dark sense of humor. Or maybe it was usually. He turned to Tara. "Are you going?"

"I was thinking about it. She was rather…adamant. Insisting we come."

"We?" Holt didn't miss a thing.

Tara cleared her throat. "I told her you would be there," she quipped, grabbing her sandwich, scooping up her prized jeans and heading for the stairs. "Don't be late. There will be forfeits."

"Of course. And Tara…" The high, slightly panicked tone of Holt's voice on her name stopped her in her tracks.

"Yes?"

"Bella's in the green room." Oh crap. And then, at her horrified expression, "She's…on timeout."

She nodded and blew out a breath, mentally thanking him for the warning.

The last thing she wanted was to walk in on Bella in a compromising position again.

Once a weekend was plenty, thank you very much.

Tara didn't sleep much that night. Her mind kept drifting back to that amazing ride with Devlin and for some reason, her pulse would start to pound and her body got all warm and she had to take care of business.

Thank God she had her own room. Hopefully she didn't wake anyone with her moaning.

The third time she woke up from a scorching dream with a burning hunger, it became a little annoying. Honestly. It was only a tryst. With a guy. She'd had trysts with guys before and walked away with absolutely no residual lust.

But they weren't Devlin, a voice whispered in her head.

She told it to shut up.

He was just a guy. Like any other guy.

Okay, he was hotter than any other guy. And he smelled better. And the low thrum of his voice as he whispered in her ear kick-started something deep in her core...but there was no reason to moon. She hated mooning. She never mooned.

Though, when she thought about it, she had to admit, it had been phenomenal. Phenomenal enough to want more. One more fling.

Too bad it wasn't going to happen.

Fucking him again would only encourage him.

Best to put him from her mind altogether.

Yet, for some reason, when she woke up, he was there, lingering in the mists of her dreams, teasing her sanity. It put her in a seriously bad mood.

She yanked on a t-shirt and some jeans and padded downstairs, delighted to see no one else was up yet. She made the coffee and an omelet and then, because she knew it would get eaten, fried up a pan of bacon. Then she took her breakfast out on the deck, sat at the patio table and stared at the sea.

It was a beautiful morning. The gentle fingers of dawn painted the water in soft orange and yellow. The evergreens on the shore swayed in the gentle breeze. Tiny sandpipers chased the waves, dancing along the surf line. It was peaceful and quiet.

It was a benefit to being a baker, she supposed, that one could get up early enough to enjoy the sunrise, and still feel as if one had languorously slept in.

"Morning." Holt's voice was gruff with sleep. Or perhaps he'd been growling at Bella all night. Tough to tell.

"Morning."

He pulled out a chair and plopped down beside her and cradled his coffee mug in his hands. "What a view."

"It is beautiful, isn't it?"

He grunted and took a sip. She glanced at him. He had *sleepy face*, which she found adorable on a man, especially a man as handsome as Holt. His eyes were half-open and a little blurred, there was a pillow crease on his beard-speckled cheek and his muscles had a softness that was not present in his usual demeanor. She wondered what Devlin's sleepy face looked like, then caught herself and forcibly thrust the thought away.

"It's always a thrill, coming here," she said, just to have something to say. Something to fill the moment. She did not expect his attention to snap to her, to fixate on her, the way it did.

"Why don't you come more often?"

God. She shouldn't have said anything.

"I come often enough."

"No. You don't. I think I've seen you twice in the past year."

She shrugged. Studied her mug. It was empty. Damn. "I need more coffee." She pushed back from the table but he stopped her. Caught her wrist in a warm grasp.

"Why *don't* you come more often?"

She blew out a laugh. "I have a job, Holt."

"We all have jobs."

"I have a *business*."

The screen door opened and Bella came out onto the deck, carrying a mug and a plate piled with the pastries Tara brought and, of course, bacon. For a self-proclaimed vegan, she ate a lot of bacon. She caught Tara mid-scowl. "Well, don't you look chipper this morning," she said, setting her plate on the table.

She and Holt shared a kiss, which was a relief because it meant he would get distracted and drop this uncomfortable topic.

But she was wrong. Once Bella sat beside him, he snagged a slice of bacon and continued. "So you have a business. How does that keep you away? If you love it here, how could that keep you away?"

She forced a saccharine smile. "Are you saying you miss me, Holt?"

He held up his hands. "Hey. I'm just curious, is all. We all come pretty regularly—except Patrick, who has good reason—and *you*."

She stared at him, lips working. Couldn't help it. What was he talking about? She wasn't one of them. She wasn't a Dawg. She was an interloper, here because one of them had so graciously invited her.

"Yeah," Bella chirped, crunching into a chocolate croissant. "Why don't you come more often? And why didn't you bring more cream puffs?"

Holt's arched brow provoked her, so Tara snapped, "Because I'm not one of you, that's why."

His eyes narrowed. "You *are*."

"I'm not on the lease, Holt."

"So?" This he said as though it made no difference at all that she had no legal right to squat here with impunity.

"So. I'm not part of the *clan*." She was on the outside looking in. She knew it. He knew it. *Everybody* knew it.

"We're hardly a clan." Bella licked some chocolate off the side of her hand.

"Just a group of people, who happen to like each other, who happen to like spending time together." He shifted in his seat, his intensity swelling. His sleepy face was definitely gone. "Are you saying you don't feel comfortable coming here?"

"I feel very comfortable coming here, Holt. Don't make this into some big *hoo-de-do-dah*."

"I'm not making this into some big *hoo-de-do-dah*."

Bella leaned in. "What's a *hoo-de-do-dah*?"

"But I absolutely would feel uncomfortable coming here without an invitation."

"Why?"

Why? "Because it's not my house."

"That's stupid." She could smack Bella. Really, she could.

"What's stupid?" Egads. Was everyone coming out here? Tara turned to see Lane, still in his pajama bottoms, leaning in the doorway. "Is that bacon?" Despite Bella's attempt to hide the plate, he grabbed a slice and though she pouted, she let him have one. One. "What's stupid?" he repeated.

Holt waved a hand in Tara's direction. "Did you know the reason she hasn't been coming is because she doesn't feel welcome?"

"I didn't say that!"

"Why doesn't she feel welcome?"

"Because she's not on the lease."

Seriously? "I'm sitting right here."

Lane gaped at her, a puzzled frown. "You're not on the lease?"

"How can you not know who's on the lease? It's your goddamn lease!" Honestly. Sometimes Lane was such a doofus.

He shrugged. "I don't pay attention to stuff like that. I have people for that." It must be nice to have people. It must be nice being richer than Croesus. "But if it'll make you feel better, we'll put you on the lease."

"Yeah," Bella winked. "And you can start paying your share of the utilities."

"Bella," Holt warned.

"She does spend a lot of time in the fridge."

"I do not!"

"Why is everyone out here?" Kristi asked, stepping onto the deck with Cam following close behind. Really? Everyone?

Yes. Everyone. Because here came Drew, rubbing the sleep from his eyes and yawning widely. "What's going on?" he asked. "Why is everyone out on the deck?"

"Did you know Tara's not on the lease?" Bella asked.

Drew blinked. "I thought we added her years ago."

Holt shook his head. "She's not on the lease."

"Well hell." Drew scrubbed his spiky hair. The Dalmatian tattoo on his bicep bulged. "We need to get her on the lease. Stat. I need you to come more often, Tara."

"You do?" His woebegone expression was adorable. The batted lashes, probably unnecessary. But she appreciated his playfulness. It cut the tension. "You need me?"

"I would die without your pastries."

"Oh my God. Me too." Cam eyed Bella's plate.

"I'll have my lawyer take care of it on Monday and bring the paperwork by for you to sign."

A heat rose on her cheeks. "No, Lane. I… You don't have to do that." Hell. This show of solidarity for her was welcoming enough. Unfamiliar. Uncomfortable, maybe. But damn nice.

"Tara." *Da-ham*. Holt could be authoritative when he put his mind to it. Her name rumbled on the skeins of the wind, as though he'd used *The Voice*. "You are one of us. You belong here. You will sign the lease."

"Sign the lease," Drew chanted, and, of course, the others joined in. The doofuses. Doofii. Whatever. She freaking loved them.

"Do you promise to sign the lease?" Holt asked. "Do you?"

"Yes Holt. I will." she said, fluttering her lashes, because playing it off like a joke was the only way she could deal with the depth of her emotion. The only way she could keep tears from dribbling down her cheek.

"Excellent."

She picked up her mug and said, with a gruff grunt, "I need more coffee." But before she could escape, Kristi stopped her with a hug. "What was that for?"

Kristi grinned. "I'm proud of you."

"Proud of me? For what?"

"You're signing the lease." Did she need to smirk like that?

"And?"

"And that, my dearest friend, is a commitment. Not a huge commitment, but definitely a step in the right direction."

Tara pursed her lips, but didn't say anything. Kristi was having fun teasing her and she didn't want to ruin the moment. But when Holt hugged her too, things got a little awkward. On account of Bella's glower.

But he made it better when he whispered in her ear, "For the record, Tara, as far as we're concerned, you have always been one of us."

CHAPTER EIGHT

Tara made it a point to get to Avery's party early on Saturday. She'd seen the kinds of forfeits Avery could deal out and she wanted no part of them. Of all her friends, only Bella and Holt were brave enough to accompany her. Bella was even kind enough to lend her something with a little kink to wear so she would fit in.

Lane and Drew claimed to have very important business to attend to, which was the coward's way of saying Avery's parties were a little too wild for their delicate sensibilities, but Cam and Kristi had been far more blunt. They had plans to canoodle.

What a shocker.

Avery and her friend Mel greeted them at the door. Avery wore a sparkly tiara festooned with little pink penises. And though they were early, the party was in full swing. Apparently no one wanted to be the last to arrive. The great room thrummed with music. Couples danced and chatted and sipped. It seemed like a regular party—just like any other party.

Tara knew better.

At some point the action would move down into the basement, into the dungeon. That's when things would get really wild.

That was probably when she'd slip out.

Though Avery had expressly invited Devlin too, Tara knew he wasn't coming. The expression on his face had made his intentions crystal clear. The thought depressed her a little—because a part of her really wanted to see him again. And maybe fuck him again.

She told that part of her to shut up.

It was a relief not having to worry about seeing him again.

It was.

"Hello darlings!" Avery cooed, giving Tara a hug. She hugged Bella and Holt as well. Holt got a little more than a hug. In fact, it took a scorching glower from Bella to put the kibosh on Avery's groping. Fortunately Holt had a lot to grope. And he didn't seem to mind. When she was finished manhandling him, she turned to Tara. "Where's your lover?"

Perhaps it was the lurid tone with which Avery said the word, or the hot rush that flooded Tara's cheeks, but something snagged Bella's attention and she gored Tara with an accusatory stare. "Your *lover*? You didn't tell me you had a boyfriend."

"I don't have a boyfriend."

"I thought you were on hiatus."

"I am."

Avery tipped her head to the side. "What is this hiatus of which you speak?"

Tara crossed her arms and glared at them all. Holt's grin did not amuse her.

"She's gone off men." Hell. Why did Bella have to put it that way? In front of Mel? Mel, who perked up like a beagle offered a slice of crispy bacon.

"Gone off men?" She sidled closer.

"Not like that," Tara muttered. "I'm taking a break."

"Hmm." Avery tapped her plush lips with a finger. "Didn't seem like that last night."

"What?" Bella screeched. She whirled on Holt. "Did you know about this? Why am I always the last one to know about stuff like this?"

Tara bristled. "It's nothing!"

"I saw the way he looked at you, sweetheart." Avery cooed. "It wasn't nothing."

"It was a game of pool. That's it. Nothing more. A. Game. Of. Pool."

Clearly, Avery wasn't buying Tara's denial. Neither was Mel, but they exchanged a mischievous glance and let the topic drop.

"Here," Mel said, handing each of them a party hat. "Put these on. And don't peek."

"Don't peek?"

Mel pointed to her hat, an itty bitty top hat set at an improbable angle. There was a small card attached to it that said *Marquis de Sade*. "The game is, you have to find your partner." Her long silver lashes fluttered as she winked.

Holt pulled Bella closer. "I have my partner."

Avery rolled her eyes with a huge sigh. "You're no fun, Holt." She turned to Mel and grumbled, "Give them both A. N. Roquelaure."

Mel pouted. "I don't want to give them both A. N. Roquelaure. They have to play the game like everyone else."

Holt growled and Mel reluctantly handed over their hats. But she deliberately thrust the pink princess cone with the flowing veil at Holt, and gave Bella the police hat. Bella was adorable in it, but of course, Holt switched them out. Tara had to admit, Holt looked much better as a sexy cop, especially dressed as he was in full leathers. Bella wore a matching outfit of tight leather pants and a sexy bustier, with a delicate jeweled collar. A perfect pair. And there was no doubt they were together.

For her part, Tara had worn her usual uniform of jeans and a blouse, but in a concession to the party theme, and thrown on Bella's tightly nipped corset. It was enough to make her look the part, without all the added aggravation of wearing latex. Which she would never borrow from Bella anyway. Or anyone, for that matter.

"Here's yours," Mel said, setting a fluffy pair of bunny ears on her head.

"Bunny ears?" she squeaked. "Seriously?"

Mel snickered and taped a card to one of the ears. "Here you go. You have to mill around in the crowd and find your partner by asking yes or no questions about your card. There's a prize for the first five pairs who find their mate. Except for you two because you're cheating." She waggled a finger at Bella and Holt.

"We're not cheating," Holt muttered. "We're not even playing."

Mel ignored him. "And, of course, a punishment for those who come in last."

Tara glanced at her friends. She frowned when they both read her card and broke out laughing. "What?" she snapped.

"Nothing." Holt scrubbed his lips, but the smile remained. Bella studied the ceiling and whistled.

Bastards.

"Well? What are you waiting for?" Avery said. "Go on in. Mingle.

Have fun!"

"And no cheating," Mel trilled.

"I hate this shit," Tara muttered as they made their way across the airy great room toward the bar.

"At least it's entertaining," Holt said with a smirk.

Tara studied the assemblage. And yeah, it was entertaining. Men and women—and ones she wasn't quite sure about—mingled and danced and laughed. Elves, sailors, firemen…even a guy in a fedora. All trying to get a peek at someone's card. Some were in a clear frenzy to find their partner—and avoid Avery's punishments. Though some were looking for a partner of another kind.

Avery typically opened her whole house for these parties. All of the rooms upstairs were available if a couple—or more than a couple—were so inclined. Most of the rooms had themes.

By midnight there would be a tangle of limbs somewhere—guaranteed.

Tara would be long gone by midnight.

If there was one saving grace at Avery's parties, it was the fact she knew how to set up an excellent bar. Then again, when one played the kinds of games Avery and Mel preferred, it helped to get their guests a little drunk. Or a lot drunk.

Tara gestured to the bartender, a pretty boy slave dressed in a leather harness, vinyl underwear—and little else. "Gin," she said. "Straight." When he delivered it, she tossed it back and requested another.

"You better go find your partner," Bella said. "Before you're too plastered to form a question."

"Why don't you just tell me who I am?"

Bella chuckled. "What makes you think you're a person?"

"Am I a person?"

Holt snorted. "Sort of."

Bella smacked him. And then they both laughed.

It annoyed the crap out of Tara that they were in on a joke and she wasn't. So she took her drink and plowed into the crowd, determined to find her stupid partner and end this stupid game.

She'd determined she wasn't a spreader bar, a pair of handcuffs, a triskelion or O fairly quickly by walking up to people with those designations and simply asking if her card matched what she read on theirs. Mel would probably count that as cheating, but Tara didn't care. It was, after all, a stupid game.

She was talking to Jonathan, a tall, slender guy in a cowboy hat who was looking for another *squick* when she saw *him*, standing there in the foyer, so tall and broad and staring directly at her. Of course he'd scored a sexy hat. And what was sexier than devil ears? Talk about appropriate. He was the very devil.

Her pulse leapt at the sight of him, her clit thrummed in an unbearable tattoo. It exasperated her, her response to him. If only her body would listen to her brain. She was not—*not*—in the market for a man. Flings led to relationships and relationships led to complications.

What she needed now was to focus on building her business.

Devlin Fox would not be helpful in that department.

Three burps proved that.

Three frickin burps.

Deliberately, she turned away and fixed her attention on the cowboy *squick*, though the words he was saying only hummed in her ears.

He was here.

She hadn't expected him to come.

Then again, she had. Perhaps, in her heart of hearts, she'd hoped he would. Maybe that was why she'd decided to brave the whips and chains she knew were in her future…or someone's future.

And surely he wasn't even more magnificent than she recalled? It had only been a day since she'd seen him. A day since he'd buried himself deep within her, thrusting and panting and painting pleasure on her every nerve.

Unable to resist, she shot a peek in his direction.

The moment their eyes met, he started toward her. Like a heat seeking missile.

Her heart stuttered. Her body flooded. Her muscles locked. She couldn't move. She felt like a gazelle on the broad Serengeti, stalked by a lion, paralyzed by the anticipation of the coming onslaught and unable to escape. Unwilling to flee. Her destiny marched toward her through the milling throng of pirates and puppy dogs—and every other presence, every other voice in the room receded.

"Hi there." An irritating buzz to her left. "Am I a switch?"

Tara blinked and turned to the fellow who had sidled up to her in Jonathan's stead. Apparently *he* had given up on her. This guy was tall and thickly muscled, shaved bald and covered with tattoos. Also, he was dressed in full leathers. In her experience, guys who came to Avery's parties in leathers were either Doms or wanna-be-doms. Regardless, the bobbling Martian antennae ruined the effect. "I beg your pardon?"

"My card. Does it say switch?" He leaned closer. "Cause I would be a switch for you."

Oh God. He was coming on to her. Her stomach heaved. She wasn't sure if it was humor, revulsion or keen anticipation. She could *feel* Devlin moving closer, as though they were connected by a vibrating thread. She forced herself to focus on this guy's card. It said *Master.* "Ah, no. You are not a switch."

He winked. "No problem. We can work it out. Do you...ah...wanna go upstairs?"

"Up...stairs?" Shit. He didn't waste any time. Too bad she wasn't in the market for an alien Dom.

A heavy arm fell over her shoulders. "Sorry dude," Devlin's deep voice rumbled in her ear. "She's my switch."

The Martian's gaze flicked from Devlin's card to hers and his hopeful expression crumbled. "Sorry man. I didn't realize she was taken." He melted back into the crowd, antennae bobbing.

Tara turned to Devlin. Her attention flicked up to his card. *Switch.* Her lips twitched. "Am I a switch?" she asked, though she knew. At least she was pretty sure.

"I dunno," he grinned. "Are you?"

She smacked him gently on the shoulder. He'd dressed for the party, but barely. Jeans and a t-shirt seemed to be his standard attire. "Does my card say *Switch*?"

"Yes ma'am."

She glanced at Avery, who was watching them from the bar and not bothering to hide her smirk. She lifted her glass, *the bitch.* "I guess we're partners then."

His grin broadened. "I guess we are."

"Judging from Avery's glee, this will be mortifying."

"As well it should be."

She nodded at his jean-clad legs. "I see you found another pair."

"I packed extras."

She nibbled her lip. "I, ah, hope you can keep these on."

"I don't." His smile was infectious. Then the playful mood

between them shifted into something darker. He leaned in and whispered, "Why did you leave?"

She turned away, staring at the partygoers, seeing nothing. She shrugged. "Wanted to avoid that whole awkward walk-of-shame thing."

He tipped her chin back, met her eyes. "There's no shame in what we did. In fact, it was fucking phenomenal."

"Was it?" She regretted her flippant tone immediately as pain flashed over his features.

"It was for me."

"Oh, all right," she grumbled. "It was pretty fucking phenomenal."

"I wanted to do it again."

So had she. Not that she'd admit it to him. She shrugged. "It was fun. I guess."

Though she wasn't looking at him, she could feel the heat of his gaze. "You still owe me, you know."

She froze. "What?"

"Peanut butter. Remember?"

She swallowed. Of course she remembered.

"But I'll settle for your name."

She flicked one of her ears. "Call me Thumper."

His eyes narrowed. "I'm serious. I can find it out myself, but I'd like for you to tell me."

They stood there, amid a sea of revelers, staring at each other. Tension thrummed between them.

She opened her mouth—surely not to tell him her name—when a loud hum, then a screech, rocked the room.

"Hello? Hello? Can you hear me?" A scratchy voice reverberated off the windows—only several hundred decibels too loud for human tolerance.

"Shit," a bumble bee muttered. "Someone gave Avery a mic."

"Hello everyone! And welcome to my fifth annual twenty-first birthday party!" A cheer rounded the room. "Has everyone found your partner?" A chorus of yeses, mingling with a couple nos, rose. "Right then. Everyone who's found your partner, head on down to the dungeon. And you poor un-partnered souls..." She chuckled evilly. "You remain here to get suited up."

"Holy crap," Tara breathed, shooting a horrified glance at Devlin.

"Suited up for what?"

He shrugged and guided her to the stairs. "It's probably better not to ask."

An exhilarating relief—that she'd found her partner before the game ended—rocketed through her.

She was sure that's what it was.

What else could it be?

CHAPTER NINE

Avery, being the bossy boots she was, made all the 'losers,' dressed as ponies, stand at the back of the room—the room being her dungeon, buried deep in the basement of her mansion. She directed the 'winners' of the game to stand in a line at the front by the fireplace.

The lights were dim. Music thrummed in a low and heady beat. It was a large open space, punctuated with all the toys of her beloved lifestyle.

Tara had seen them all before. A St. Andrew's Cross, a swing, wall manacles…but she'd never seen them festooned with party streamers and condom balloons. It did not make them less intimidating.

She comforted herself with the knowledge that even Avery would not force one of her partygoers to slip into the diabolical leather straitjacket hanging from a hook on the wall.

Then again…

"Okay everyone!" Avery crowed, clearly in her element. "It's time for prizes. These clever pairs all found their partners first…" She waved at the ten of them standing in a row. "Each one of you win a prize. We'll start with the gentlemen." She carried a velvet bag down the line, urging the men to reach in and pull out a ball.

Christoff was the first to draw. He pulled out a red ball, read it and chuckled. "Spanking," he announced.

Avery winked. "Well, it is my birthday. You knew there would be some spankings in there." She affected a pout. "I deserve my presents too. Okay Christoff. You may select the partygoer of your choice and administer five spanks. If you choose one of the losers you can double the spanks."

A groan rose from the stable.

Christoff grinned. He fixated on Thomas, one of the ponies, who blushed crimson. Christoff sat on the big wooden throne—which was actually a bondage chair, judging from the leather straps on the arms—and patted his knee. The assemblage laughed as Thomas made his way over, trotting when Avery so commanded, and draped himself over Christoff's lap. Christoff gleefully administered ten swats, accompanied by the chanted counts from the crowd.

When he stood, Thomas' cheeks were red, but the look he sent Christoff was more scorching yet.

"Next!" Avery bellowed, holding up the bag for Jonathan—the cowboy. He pulled out a green ball which, he read, entitled him to a foot rub from the guest of his choice. His gaze rounded the room. When it settled on Tara, her belly lurched. Not that she didn't like cowboys, but the thought of giving any guy a foot rub grossed her out. Because, in her experience, men could be very casual about changing their socks.

But when Devlin bristled and sent a fulminating frown down the line, Jonathan's attention moved on and settled on Mel. "You," he said.

Mel sputtered for a moment, but after a nudge from Avery she met Jonathan by the throne. She set her hands on her hips and barked, "Okay. Sit down."

But Jonathan didn't sit down. He took Mel by the shoulders, angled her onto the throne and knelt at her feet. "The prize is a foot rub," he said with a wink. "It doesn't say I have to receive one."

Mel's mood shifted immediately. A grin wreathed her face and she kicked off her bejeweled sandals. "Well, in that case," she murmured, burying her foot in his lap.

The foot rub went on for far too long—who knew Jonathan had a foot fetish? And while Mel didn't complain, Avery did.

When Jonathan proved loath to relinquish his prize, Avery moved on to the next man in line. Andy pulled a blue ball. Everyone in the room groaned—every guy. They knew what a blue ball meant.

"Lap dance!" Avery chanted, and everyone joined in.

Andy chose Bella for his lap dance, which wasn't very bright, because Holt stood over them as Bella performed; she ruthlessly gyrated on Andy while sending teasing looks over her shoulder at her man. Needless to say, the lap dance didn't last too long.

Probably on account of Holt's snarling.

And then Avery sidled up to Devlin, the last man in the lineup.

Horror suffused Tara as Devlin reached into the velvet bag and pulled out a red ball. She knew, she just knew, what it said. Spanking. And she knew who he'd pick.

His lips quirked. He surveyed the room as though he were weighing the options. He stalled on Bella but, Tara suspected, only to get a rise out of Holt. It worked. Devlin chuckled and continued his leisurely perusal.

Her heart shouldn't have been thudding like that. There was no reason to be so excited… Then it stopped altogether for a brief, painful moment. His gaze pierced her, goring her to her core. And he quirked his finger.

Damn.

She shouldn't have come. She knew she shouldn't have come. At the same time, the thought of being draped over those tree-like thighs, the thought of his broad palm on her ass, made her go hot then cold then hot again. The little hairs at her nape prickled. Her body liquefied.

She hardly even noticed the cheer going up around the room. Hardly noticed Avery's chortle.

In a fog, she crossed the room and met him at the throne. He sat.

Yeah. It was too much to ask that *he* might want to receive the spanking.

"Five swats," Avery instructed.

Tara glowered at her and started to arrange herself over Devlin's lap. "Hold on," he whispered. "I think you need to pull down your jeans."

She gaped at him. "What?" In front of everyone?

He shrugged. "It's *my* prize."

"I get a prize too," she snapped. "Don't forget that."

Her threat did not seem to faze him. "Bring it on, baby," he said.

Oooh, would she.

Rather than let her mortification show, she decided to play it up, shimmying her jeans over her hips in a sexy little dance. Devlin's nostrils flared as he watched. When she draped herself over his lap, she made it a point to nudge his cock. It was hard. Hard as a rock.

Excellent. She was going to tease him silly tonight—

The first smack surprised her.

She hadn't expected it to be so sharp. She cried out in protest, but the sound was drowned out by the cheers of the crowd. "One!" they bellowed through laughs and catcalls.

The second fell and a heat consumed her. A heat separate from the burning imprint of his hand on her ass. That he slowly stroked and soothed the spot afterwards didn't help.

At the third, arousal bubbled in her belly. The sheer roiling power of it stunned her. She'd been spanked before, by boys playing a similar game. But her reaction had never been so feral. Again his palm skidded slowly over her stinging skin.

With the fourth came a hunger. A raging fever of desire. She wiggled against Devlin, pressing into the firm bulge by her hip. He hissed in a breath. His fingers tightened on her ass. She thought she heard a whimper.

She could have been mistaken, but she was sure she wasn't.

She glanced over her shoulder and their eyes met, just as the fifth smack fell. And something happened between them. It was like an electric wire, live and humming and charged with lust. She wanted him. In her. And she wanted him now.

She started to lever off his lap, but he pressed her back down and quickly landed two more swats. "Hey!" she cried, but Devlin only chuckled as he helped her stand and pull up her jeans. She wrenched away and fastened them herself, hiding the unholy flush on her face.

Damn.

How could he do this to her? Seven simple swats on her ass and she was ready to drag him into a back bedroom and fuck him silly.

She made it a point to take her place in line…far away from him.

Avery moved on to her next victim, Angela, who scored a slave collar to bestow on the attendee of her choice. She chose the Martian, which made Tara laugh. Because he looked mighty amusing in his Dom leathers wearing a collar and, apparently, *glow-in-the-dark* antennae.

A few more spankings were bestowed as Avery made her way down the line, joking that she fully intended to get all her licks in. Tara hoped to hell she pulled a red ball, so she could give Devlin his just desserts. She was bound for disappointment.

She pulled a blue one.

"Another lap dance," Avery announced. "Who's it going to be?" she asked with a wink. Although her expression made clear she knew the answer.

Tara tried to bite back a naughty grin as she turned to Devlin. Although she didn't try very hard. "You," she said, pointing straight at him.

His enthusiasm was comical. But not as comical as the way his jaw dropped when *she* sat on the throne. "I want you to give me a lap dance."

"What?" A squeak.

"And…" she waggled her fingers at his chest. "Take off that shirt."

He glowered at her as he complied, but she could see the flame in his eyes. As he peeled off his shirt, all the women in the room, and some of the men, hooted and whistled. He leaned in close. "You know I'm going to get you back for this," he muttered.

She winked. "I'm counting on it."

But what she wasn't counting on was how damn good he was at lap dances.

He started off slowly swaying his hips from side to side, gyrating in a motion that left nothing to the imagination. The bulge in his tight jeans snagged her attention. Made her mouth water. Made her imagination wander.

As he undulated, the tight muscles of his chest rippled.

God, he was hot. He could be a stripper…if he wanted to.

Then he reached out one arm toward her.

And the other.

Touched his neck with one hand.

And the other.

When he crossed his arms over his hips she laughed out loud, realizing exactly what dance he was doing.

"A real lap dance," she insisted.

"This is a real lap dance." He continued doing the Macarena until he reached the hip swizzle. Then he got serious. He moved closer, hovering over her, brushing his chest over hers and breathing into her hair.

Setting his hands on her knees, he spread her legs. She tried to resist, really she did, but she couldn't.

Heat scorched her as he plastered against her and slithered down her body. He was hot and transferred that heat to her in that long slow slide. He moved against her, easing downward, until he buried his face in her lap.

She didn't imagine the little nip he gave her on the inside of her thigh, but if she had, the naughty grin he sent her would have convinced her.

He made his way back up again, dragging his torso against hers, until his mouth found her neck.

She leaped a little when he nibbled her there, and sucked.

Lust skewered her. Oh, how she wished they were not in a room full of people. This wouldn't be a playful lap dance. It would be a bacchanal.

She couldn't help raking her fingers through his hair and holding him in place until Avery tapped her toe and sighed loudly.

"Okay, okay. We have lots more games, people," she muttered.

Still, Devlin didn't budge. "I like it here," he murmured into Tara's ear, and she laughed. Her laughter stalled when he rubbed his cock against her belly in a suggestive way.

And she was very susceptible to suggestion.

Especially this kind of suggestion.

"I need you," he said.

"Later," she whispered, very aware that everyone, including Holt and Bella, were gaping at them. Some of them drooling.

Devlin pulled back to meet her eye. "Promise?"

"Get off." She pushed at his hard, immovable chest.

"Promise first."

"Okay," she grumbled, although it wasn't a difficult promise to make. It would not be a difficult promise to keep. Another night, another fuck at least, with Devlin Fox was hardly a hardship. "I prom—"

He sealed the word with his lips. Kissing her, consuming her, seducing her with a long, leisurely exploration. He probably would have kept kissing her if Avery hadn't grabbed his arm and pulled him away. "Enough of that you two," she said. And then she added, under her breath, "Get a room."

Devlin and Tara's gazes met at the suggestion.

Avery's mansion had a plethora of rooms. Surely one of them would be empty.

Warm wet arousal bubbled. A sizzle of anticipation scorched her nerve endings.

But then she caught Holt's glower and she decided it might be a good idea to wait to scamper away…until he wasn't watching her like the proverbial hawk.

Not that Holt was her keeper. But he did fancy himself the protector of all women in his aegis—whether she wanted to be protected or not. Even though he was here with Bella, he *had* accompanied Tara to the party. He would consider himself her escort.

And as annoying as Devlin Fox could be, Tara didn't want to see him pounded into the ground.

Clearly, they needed to wait for an opportunity to sneak away.

When Avery announced the next game, *Dom Pong*—which was similar to *Beer Pong*, but with ball gags—Tara knew it was time. She waited until Bella and Holt were deeply engrossed in the game, shot a look at Devlin—who, to her annoyance had put his shirt back on—and notched her head.

His nostrils flared. He glanced at Holt and then slowly made his way to the stairs and disappeared.

After a moment, Tara followed.

It was a shock to the system to emerge from the rollicking, shadowed dungeon into the brightly lit, deserted, great room.

As she came through the door, Devlin caught her around the waist and backed her up against the wall.

His mouth was hot, hungry, savage on hers.

"God," he whispered. "I want you."

"Not here," she murmured against his lips. Because she knew if she didn't say the words, they would. Right. Here.

Her body was on fire for him and she could tell, from the hum of arousal in him, he was mad for her as well.

He continued to kiss her, moving toward the stairs leading to the upper floor. They bumped into furniture and nearly toppled a lamp in their frenzy to make it to a private space. Finally, he separated from her, took her hand and bolted up the stairs. Several of the rooms on the second floor were locked. The passionate moans and groans emanating from them only fueled their fire.

Devlin ignored the rest of the doors, continuing up to the third floor. He pulled her into the first room he found free and backed her against the wall, kicking the door closed.

They came together in a rush. A crazed scramble ensued as he unlaced her corset and pulled off her shirt as she wrestled with his. They finally gave up, and each undressed themselves, tossing their clothes into an unruly pile on the floor until they wore nothing but underwear.

He fell onto the bed, pulling her with him, fiddling with her bra snap. "Damn thing," he grumbled.

She laughed. "Let me." She sat back and reached behind her, unfastening her bra. He hissed in a breath when her breasts tumbled free.

"Jesus." He captured each globe in a hand and brought them to his mouth, one after the other, drawing them in with long, lingering sucks.

She shivered. The heat of his hands on her flesh was invigorating. His touch set her afire. She angled a knee over his torso and straddled him, encouraging him to feast. As he did, she explored his shoulders, his bulging biceps with trembling fingers. Unable to resist, she scored his back with her nails.

He growled and buried his face in her cleavage. "God. God." He leaned back and pulled her on top of him, settling her groin on his. The pressure of his erection was nearly painful. She rubbed against him like a cat, massaging her thrumming clit through their underwear.

As she did so, she kissed the underside of his chin and, liking the taste of him, lapped. He shivered. She scooted lower, kissing and stroking his chest, nibbling on his nipples until he wheezed a plea of some kind. She had no idea for what he begged—or perhaps a small idea. She continued lower, licking and lapping his magnificent cut abs, exploring them with such devilish attention he began to writhe.

They both knew where this was heading, but she was determined to make him suffer. Her ass still burned from the spanking he'd given her.

She would have her mouth on him soon—just not too soon.

When she reached the band of his underwear, she traced his cock. Thick. Full. Throbbing. It jerked at her touch. She glanced up at him to see him staring at her with glittering eyes. His Adam's apple worked. She grinned and exhaled a hot breath over him.

He threw back his head with a groan. "Ah…baby…"

Slowly she eased down his underwear, exposing his cock. Her pulse surged. It was beautiful. Simply beautiful. Her mouth watered.

She swallowed heavily. She took him in her fist and stroked.

"I'm sorry, Devlin," she murmured.

He jerked up. "What?" he squawked. "Sorry for what?"

The look she sent him was scorching. "Sorry that I don't have any peanut butter," she said. And then she took him in her mouth.

CHAPTER TEN

Devlin's muscles locked. His breath escaped in a harsh rush. His pulse jerked.

Tara's lips encased him and she nibbled the swollen head of his cock.

Delight skittered up his spine. Insanity clouded his brain.

Jesus, God she was beautiful, perfect.

She took him deeper, dragging her velvety mouth over his glans, burying him in her throat. Her muscles worked him as she made her way up and down and up again. Then she took up a heinous rhythm, fucking him with her mouth, her fist playing a fiendish counterpoint along his length. He fought back a shiver, but it took him when her hand twisted around his length in a corkscrew motion, when her finger slid along his sensitive flesh to toy with his ass.

"Jesus," he roared, sinking his hands into her hair. Desperately trying to guide her motions. When she would not allow that, he grabbed her shoulders and hauled her up, over him. She felt so good, her weight on his body, her warmth soaking into him. He fumbled with her panties, tugging them down. "In," he said. "I need in."

She set her hand on his and stilled, meeting his gaze. "Do you…"

"What?" What? *What?*

"Do you have a condom?"

Shit. *Shit.* He'd nearly forgotten *again.* "In my jeans."

He shifted her off him, over to the side, though clearly she wanted to leap for his jeans.

But he didn't trust her around his jeans. He found them in the pile

74

on the floor and fished around until he came up with the foil packet. He ripped it open with his teeth and returned to the bed, where she crouched, watching him like a hungry lioness.

He'd had every intention of lying back down, of guiding her atop him, of watching as she sank down onto his cock and rode him, but when he saw her there like that, hair mussed, eyes wild, he knew he had to take her from behind.

"Get on your knees," he commanded as he slipped the condom onto his aching cock. A skitter of elation tore through him when she complied, presenting herself to him with knees wide. She glanced at him over her shoulder and when he didn't move quickly enough, when he didn't cover her and sink into her like a savage beast, she wiggled her ass.

He couldn't help it.

His hand came down on one fleshy globe before he could stop it. She hissed in a growl. Her expression became even steamier.

"Did you like that spanking?" he asked, kneeling on the bed behind her and setting himself to her gleaming opening.

"Yes."

He smacked her again, loving her response.

They were both feral. Like animals in the wild, mating.

He spread her cheeks and lifted her, just a tad, and sank in.

He did it slow, determined to tease her, to make her body ache for him, ache for more. Judging from her guttural groan, he hit the mark as he eased in deep. But he was teasing himself as well. He wanted to thrust. He wanted to plunge. He wanted to possess her in a wild frenzy.

But he didn't.

In. Out. In. Slow. Lazy. Languorously.

She was tight. Hot. Wet. She clenched him in a mind-boggling grip with each withdrawal. And with each withdrawal, new skeins of agony wound through his loins.

"More," she whimpered, burying her head in her arms. "More."

Oh, he gave her more.

First, a smack on the ass, hard enough that the crack resounded through the room. Hard enough that his handprint rose on her creamy cheek. Gratification flooded him at the sight.

She tightened around him as his hand fell. And he nearly lost his load right then and there. He clenched his ass to keep it in. Forced his mind to focus on holding back what his body so desperately wanted to give. Because he wanted more.

He grabbed her hips and pulled her hard against him, hunching over her so with every thrust, their bodies rubbed together. He explored her from this angle and that, looking, searching and finding what gave her the most pleasure. "You like that, baby? You like that?" he murmured in her ear as he landed one hard thrust.

"Yes. Yes."

He pulled out, nearly all the way, and then thrust home, making it a point to hit her there again, at that angle, the one that made her quiver and quake.

"Yes." She pushed back, matching his lunges with little thrusts of her own. The sound of flesh slapping flesh filled the room, punctuated by her moans and his groans.

His pace increased.

He wanted to go slow. He wanted to make her beg. But he was a weak man. Faster and faster, in greater and greater frenzy, he took her, possessed her, dominated her body with his. And she gave back everything, measure for measure.

It occurred to him, as he fucked her in a fury of mindless passion, that he'd never had a partner quite like her. Never known a woman to give as good as she got, to challenge him, to demand of him that which he was desperate to give. She was as close to perfect as a woman could ever come.

And then all thoughts flew.

All sanity.

All logic.

She came around him.

Fantastically. Her body devolved into a series of shivers and quivers and manic thrusts, milking him, stroking him, taking him right along with her.

Stiffening, shuddering, she threw back her head and wailed.

Her grip on his cock was blinding. A scorching wave overcame him. Consumed him. He erupted. Sank into a swell of bliss. Bliss twined with sizzling agony. With release, relief and…regret.

Regret that it was over.

When they were finished, still quaking in the aftermath of an all consuming orgasm, he pulled out, stripped off the condom and tossed it into the trash can, wrapped her in his arms and held her.

Simply held her, savoring the feel her soft skin against his. Counting the beats of her heart as it thudded against his. He buried his nose in her hair, breathing in her scent.

He could lay like this, stay like this, forever.

Of course, it was not forever.

Far too soon, she stirred.

He tightened his hold. "You're not leaving." A dark murmur.

To his consternation, she chuckled. "We should get back to the party."

"Not yet." He wanted to recuperate. Wanted to have her again. Before she escaped. Hopefully, not with his jeans. He dipped his head and kissed her, loving the taste of her on his tongue.

But again, she shifted. Pulled away. "We should get back."

Annoyance slithered through him. "Why?"

She wriggled from his embrace and found her bra. He hated watching her put it on. "Holt."

He shot up and frowned at her. Jealousy skewered his gut. "Holt?" She was thinking of another man? After *that*?

She chuckled at his dismay, which was irritating as hell. "He'll be wondering where I am."

Devlin couldn't hold back his snarl. "Are you and he…"

Her chuckle became a full bodied laugh. "No. Nothing like that." She found her shirt and slipped it on. And her panties. Realizing he was falling behind, he rooted around in the blankets for his underwear. "Bella would kill me if I looked at him sideways. Besides, he's always been like a brother to me."

Devlin gritted his teeth. He knew guys like Holt Lamm. *Brother* was not in their vocabulary. Not when it came to women like Ponytail. But he didn't want to fight about it. Didn't want to fight about anything. So, grudgingly he yanked on his shirt. She picked up his jeans and he gently pried them from her grip. "Not this time, sweetheart," he murmured as he tugged them on.

She smiled.

He loved her smile. Unable to resist, he pulled her into his arms. "I don't want this to be over," he said.

She stared at him. "This?"

"This thing."

"This thing?"

Was he speaking English?

"Sweetheart…"

"We should get back." She untangled herself from his hold and headed for the door. He followed, but he wasn't done. Not by a long shot. So when she opened the door, he reached over her shoulder and held it shut.

"When can I see you again?"

"Devlin." She turned and gazed up at him with a confabulating expression in her eyes. He'd always been able to read a woman. This, he could not read. Or maybe he didn't want to read it. Maybe he didn't like what it said.

It kind of felt like: *It's over.*

Fuck. He hoped not.

"Didn't you enjoy this?" He sure as shit had. It was incomprehensible to imagine she had not. He glanced at the bed, remembering her growls, her moans, the wild response of her body when he'd buried himself deep inside her.

She tipped her head to the side. "Enjoy it? Of course I did." She went up on her tiptoes and kissed him.

"Then when can I see you again?"

A shadow flickered over her features, one that made his gut curdle. "Devlin—" God he hated that tone. "I'm not…in the market for a relationship."

He stepped back and crossed his arms over his chest. "I'm not proposing marriage."

"I know. But these things have a way of…evolving into something more."

Something more sounded great. Something more sounded fan-fucking-tabulous. He wanted her…but having her on her terms would work for him. "What if we make a pact?"

Her brows knit. "What kind of pact?"

"No relationship."

"Just…fuck buddies?"

Discomfort drizzled through him. "If that's that you want to call it. Sure."

"No emotions? No crazy jealousy? No stalking?"

He forced a laugh. "What kinds of guys have you been dating?"

She blew out a breath. "You know what I mean. I have a busy life. I don't have time for…drama."

"Drama?" He glanced at the bed again. Had that been drama?

Why did women have to be so damn inscrutable?

"You know. Jealousy. Possessiveness. Demands on my time."

Her words rang through him with an eerie familiarity. He knew them well. He'd said them himself. Many times before. He'd been a player most of his adult life, dating girl after girl. Like a horny bee flittering from one flower to the next. He'd never liked drama in a relationship. Never liked when *she* got jealous or possessive or started checking his cell phone for messages. That was usually when he ended it.

It had never bothered him before—ending it.

But now he was faced with this. This woman, spouting the same idiotic philosophy.

And it was...idiotic.

She wanted a fuck buddy. Someone who would show up for a booty call, give her what she wanted and then quietly leave.

Oddly enough, the prospect irritated the hell out of him.

Because suddenly, incomprehensibly, he wanted more.

And he wanted more with her.

And while he would do just about anything to be with her, to his astonishment, he realized he didn't think he could offer her that.

For some reason the thought of nothing but casual sex with this woman—whose name he did not know—sent a piercing shaft of pain through his heart.

CHAPTER ELEVEN

He'd said no.

Tara stumbled over a root as she followed Bella and Holt up the path back home, her mind awhirl. She was thankful for the shadows. She didn't think she could explain away the tears on her cheeks.

He'd said no.

Even though it had been his idea in the first place. Or had it? She thought back to their conversation but couldn't remember it clearly. All she could see in her mind's eye was his face as, all of a sudden his smile had faded, his brow had knit and he'd said, *"No. I don't think so."*

And why the hell did it bother her so much? It was what she'd wanted, wasn't it? To fuck him and walk away?

Surely there wasn't a teeny tiny part of her that had expected him to bristle and say, *"No. Damn it woman. I want you and you alone."* And then maybe pull her back into his arms and ravage the shit out of her.

But he hadn't.

Quietly, gently, devastatingly, he'd said, "No. I don't think so. I can't be your fuck buddy." And then he'd tenderly laced up her corset, kissed her on the forehead and left.

She should be happy. She should be delighted. She should be delirious with glee. She'd gotten her itch scratched by the hottest man on the planet and walked away unscathed, unfettered. Absolutely free of him.

Her mood sank deeper at the thought.

Holt tossed a glance at her over his shoulder. "So what's the deal with you and Devlin?" he asked.

Tara glared at him, though he could hardly see it through the darkness. "Nothing."

Bella blew out a laugh, winding her arm around Holt's. "It hardly looked like nothing when he was giving you that lap dance."

"It was nothing."

"And where did you and Devlin go off to?"

"Off too?" Why didn't they both just shut up?

"Yeah." Holt slowed and waited for her to catch up as the path widened enough for them to walk three abreast. She was hardly appreciative. "We finished the Dom Pong and you were gone."

Damn him. She used to think his protective streak was cute. Not anymore. "I'm a grown up, Holt."

"But I thought you didn't like him," Bella murmured. "You said he was a douche." Her nose wrinkled. "Didn't he give your bakery a bad review or something?"

"There's nothing between us." The words came out sharper than she intended.

Bella fell silent and then, after a moment, murmured. "It didn't look like nothing. When he was giving you that lap dance."

"Will you please stop talking about the lap dance? It was only a game."

Bella didn't respond. But Tara didn't miss the frowns she and Holt exchanged.

No one spoke again until they reached the deck of their place. Holt nodded to Bella to go on in, but he snagged Tara's arm as she tried to pass.

"What?" she snapped.

"Nothing much, Tara," he murmured. "Just, if that douche hurt you, I will rip him apart."

"He didn't hurt me, Holt," she said, wrenching free and slipping past him through the slider.

In order for Devlin to hurt her, she had to have feelings for him. And she didn't.

Not at all.

Not hardly at all.

And the fact that she couldn't stop thinking about him had nothing to do with the fact he'd said no.

Nothing at all.

Really.

* * *

On Monday it was back to the grind. Tara went to bed early on Sunday so she could face three am, but she found herself tossing and turning and—most annoyingly—thinking about Devlin. Replaying their trysts in her mind. Over and over.

It aggravated her that she was mooning over him. She'd never mooned over a man in her life. She resolved to put him from her thoughts.

But that turned out to be more difficult than she'd anticipated.

As she stood next to Jose at the butcher's block, rolling out pastry dough, she found herself reflecting on Devlin's chin, and that rough burn of scruff that had felt so exquisite scraping over her nipples. And later, as she whipped up royal icing, she imagined what his cock would look like, slathered in the stuff. How delicious it would be to lap it off.

Later still, when the shop was open, and she was serving her usual morning customers, she'd caught a glimpse of a sandy brown head of spiky hair from the corner of her eye and her heart had skipped a beat…and then plummeted when she realized it wasn't him.

Damn it all anyway.

He was only a guy. Like every other guy she'd fucked. Why he had such a hold on her was a mystery.

She was miserable for most of the week and it pissed her off. Rather than enjoying every moment at her bakery, she found herself wishing she could be on the island. With him. *Entangled.* She wanted to pack up her things and head over there right now, but she couldn't.

She had a business to run.

Besides, there was no guarantee he would be there.

And she wasn't thinking about him.

She wasn't.

When she had a free moment and logged onto his website to read his most recent review, it wasn't because she wanted to know where he'd eaten, or how he was doing or whether or not he was thinking of her. It was stupid of her to be disappointed when there was nothing there but his usual fare, clever and acerbic comments about *Le Bon Popuet,* a pretentious French Restaurant that had opened in the SoDo District.

She hadn't expected him to revise his review of her bakery and give her more burps.

Really.

She hadn't.

So there was no reason for her to slam her laptop shut the way she did.

"T?" Jose's low voice wrenched her from her misery. She took a moment and forced a blasé smile.

"Yes?"

"You still need Louisa to cover next Wednesday?"

Tara stared at her assistant, trying to make her brain work.

"Your sister's still coming, right?"

Oh. Yeah. Tina was flying into SeaTac at nine in the morning—the bakery's busiest time. "Yes, please, if she could." Louisa, Jose's wife, had been a godsend, picking up hours here and there when Tara needed to leave the shop. She'd been thinking about bringing her on full time so Tara could concentrate more on marketing, but then business had dropped off. It was just starting to pick up again. She liked to think that had little to do with the revamped menu...which included a wide range of gluten-free offerings.

Jose tossed a towel over his shoulder and chuckled. "She loves to come in. Anytime."

"She's great with the customers." No one could up-sell a pastry like Louisa. And she wasn't bad in the baking department either. "In fact..." She checked her calendar. "Can she cover Sunday as well? I made reservations to take Tina out to dinner on Saturday." Dinner out usually meant a late night. Ten at the very least. Getting up at three would be a bear. Tara didn't eat out often, but this was a special occasion. The first birthday she and her sister had been able to share in five years.

"Sure thing." Jose winked. "I'll let her know."

"Awesome."

The bell on the door jingled and Jose leaned back to glance into the shop. He grimaced. "It's for you," he muttered. The way he slunk back into the kitchen was indicative of who their customer was.

Tara checked at the clock and winced. Five after three. She should have been paying attention. She should have been there at three on the dot to flip the sign and lock the door. She should have known.

She blew out a breath, and girding her loins, went to face her nightmare.

Chet stood in the shop, hands on his hips, pretending to survey the pastry case. Tara knew better. Sure enough, as soon as she entered the room, his head snapped up. He grinned.

He was handsome when he grinned. Well, he was always handsome, but more so when he grinned. He was tall and muscular and had a lush head of thick curls. And eyes that crinkled at the corners.

By rights, she should be swooning, but when she looked at him, she felt nothing. Oh, sure, he was great in bed. A real tiger. But that passion had burned out long ago—for her, at least. It was hard to say exactly when the relationship had ended. Probably the day she'd woken up to find him on her computer reading her emails. Or maybe the time he'd yelled at her for smiling at a male customer. *She'd been too friendly*, he'd said. Or the time he'd told her—*told her*—she couldn't go with her girlfriends to the island on a girls-only vegan weekend because he wanted to *be* with her. And then he'd spent the whole weekend on her couch playing *Call of Duty* and eating her pastries.

Or maybe it was the day he'd brought his toothbrush into her apartment.

"Chet."

"Hey baby." He came around the counter and pulled her into his arms. When he bent to kiss her, she turned her cheek.

"I thought I told you not to come here anymore."

"No one's here."

"Chet—"

"Since you get off at three, I thought maybe we could go grab a late lunch."

Get off at three? The shop closed at three. There was still a lot of work to do. "I can't."

His brow puckered. "Tara, baby. I told you I was sorry. When are you going to get over this snit thing?"

"This snit thing?"

"You know. You're pouting." He pulled her closer and nestled his crotch against hers. "I've missed you baby."

Was it wrong to notice how much less of a man he was than Devlin?

Probably not.

He was. Less of a man. In so many respects.

The realization irritated her.

She pushed back. "There is no snit. This thing is over."

"This thing?"

Oh shit. She knew that look. The one right before he started yelling.

"You need to leave."

Chet bristled. Inched closer. Tara glanced around for a weapon—should she need one. The day-olds were hard, but probably not hard enough to make a dent. What a pity she didn't have a spatula.

Jose saved the day, poking his head through the doorway, warbling in a sing-song voice, "You want I should call 9-1-1?"

Tara stepped back, away from this looming threat and crossed her arms. "Well, Chet? Should he call?" She wasn't afraid of Chet, but he did have a temper. And frankly, she didn't want to deal with the drama.

He glared from her to Jose and back again and then, muttering, "Fucking bitch," slammed out of the shop.

Tara followed him to the door and bellowed, "And don't come back." Then, with what felt like a wave of finality and relief, locked it behind him.

She turned to find Jose leaning against the doorway to the kitchen shaking his head and clucking his tongue. "Baby, you sure got bad taste in men."

Tara blew out a breath. What an understatement.

Never once had she landed a nice, normal guy.

It pissed her off that she thought of Devlin just then. He'd seemed like a nice guy. A normal guy.

But honestly…what nice, normal guy gave a woman three burps and then tried to insist it was a good thing?

It was a relief that he'd said no to her offer. It was awesome that the thing between them—whatever it had been—was over. She'd never see him again. Not ever.

And she was glad.

Truly she was.

CHAPTER TWELVE

Saturday was particularly busy. From the moment they opened there was a steady stream of customers, so Tara hardly had time to think about Devlin at all. But when she did, she realized why she was so obsessed with him, even now, a full week after their tryst.

It wasn't that he was the hottest guy she'd ever met, or the fact that his voice resonated with a spine-tingling rumble. It wasn't the cut chin, or the sculpted abs. It wasn't his smell or his taste or his presence.

It was the fact that he'd said *no*.

He'd refused her offer.

No one had ever told her no when she'd offered sex before.

No one.

That's what she couldn't wrap her brain around.

She realized how stupid it was to mope. Women got shot down on occasion, didn't they? Her friends complained to her about it all the time. But it had never happened to her.

She needed to get over it and move on.

There were lots of fish in the sea.

But…none of them were quite that cute.

Bending down to refill the marzipan pig tray, she glanced up when the bell dinged over the door. As though she had conjured him with her mind, Devlin strode into her shop. She gaped at him through the glass, marveling at how gorgeous he looked in a Mariner's jacket and jeans.

It should be illegal for a man to look that hot in a baseball jacket.

He didn't see her at first, glancing around at the cases and running his fingers through his spiky hair. When he lifted his hand, his jacket opened, revealing a black t-shirt molded to his chest. She nearly swallowed her tongue.

"Ahem." She shifted the tray and stood, pinning an enormous—fake—smile on her face. "Hi there! Can I help you?"

His attention snapped to her. His eyes widened. He grinned. "Hi there."

Oh, lord. Rumbly. Low. Seductive.

She steeled her spine. "Can I help you?" she repeated.

As he stepped closer his grin widened, but then he must have noticed her smile, and how fake it was, and his mood deflated a little. He studied the cases and stroked his chin.

She tried not to notice. The chin. The stroking. The peep of his tongue as it dabbed out to wet his lips.

"Yeah. I would like one of these." He pointed to a cream puff.

"Uh huh." She picked up a pastry box and folded it.

"And one of these." A chocolate chunk cookie. "And one of these." A caramel pecan puff pastry.

Tara nodded and picked up the tongs, snagging a cream cheese cinnamon muffin, a rice flour raisin cookie and a mini loaf of almond flour swirl, all of which she nested in wax paper. "Anything else?"

Devlin viewed the contents of the box askance. "Um… Those aren't the things I asked for."

Tara affected a vivacious smile. "I know."

He glanced back at the cream puff case. "But I really wanted one of those."

"Aw." Tara sighed heavily as she closed the box and taped it with a Stud Muffin sticker. "Too bad." She set the box on the countertop and rang up the items.

"No. Really… I wanted a cream puff." How could a grown man appear so woebegone? "And a cookie."

She waggled a finger at him and leaned closer, whispering, "Sorry. Those all have gluten in them." She patted the box. "These are all gluten-free."

He stared at her and then, as he realized what she was up to, a tiny smile tweaked his lips. "You, ah, aren't going to give me what I ordered?"

She pointed to the sign by the register that stated, *We Reserve the*

Right to Refuse Service to Anyone. She'd never had to use it before, but was damn glad it was there. There was no way Devlin Fox was getting anything from her that wasn't strictly gluten-free.

No. Freaking. Way.

"Okay." He tucked the box under his arm. "How much do I owe you?"

"Nine dollars and seventy five cents."

He whistled as he peeled a ten from his wallet. "Pretty stiff for pastries."

"They are specialty items."

He dropped a ten on the counter. "Keep the change."

She rang up the till and pulled out a quarter and dropped it purposefully into the tip jar. It hit with a clang. "Thank you sir. And…" Another saccharine smile, "Come again."

His response was so wicked it made her knees knock, and not only because of the *double entendre*, but because of the tone with which he infused them. "Oh, I will." A wink. "I'm counting on it."

With that he whirled to leave the shop. But Tara couldn't let him go, couldn't let him leave without the last word.

It was too bad she couldn't think of anything clever.

Devlin made it a point to visit his baker the next day and the next. Each day she had a new sign up by the register. First it was, *We Reserve the Right to Refuse Service to Devlin Fox.* And then, *We Reserve the Right to Serve only Gluten-free to Devlin Fox.* And each day, she gave him the damn gluten-free pastries.

Oh, they were good. They were damn good. But that was hardly the point. What he really wanted was that cream puff.

Strike that.

What he really wanted was *her.*

She had become something of a challenge to him. He would wear her down.

He would.

He wasn't sure how, but he would.

On Tuesday, when Devlin came to the shop, he brought reinforcements. Reinforcements in the form of a small boy. He was an adorable boy, with a gap-toothed smile. He was dressed just like Devlin in jeans and a Mariner's jacket. Even their spiky hair matched.

The sight tugged at Tara's heartstrings. Because they looked so much alike, it was clear they were father and son.

It had never occurred to her that he might have a child. Never occurred to her that he probably had a woman in his life. If not many.

He was far too attractive to be unencumbered.

Damn. She hadn't thought to ask if he was married. Or divorced. Or *involved*.

No wonder he'd said no.

The thought made acid boil in her belly. She didn't know why. She had no claim to him. She wanted no claim.

But still, it rankled.

"Can I help you?" She didn't even bother with the fake smile.

The boy stepped up to the counter and gazed at her with wide eyes, a puppy dog expression. "I would like a cream puff, please miss."

"A cream puff?"

"Yes, please, miss. That one." He pointed to the refrigerated case.

She glared at Devlin, who didn't bother to hide his smirk.

"How about one of these?" She said through her teeth, pointing at the gluten-free pastries.

The boy shook his head. "No, miss. That one. Please?" He folded his hands and raised them to her as though in prayer.

Good lord, the boy was a drama queen.

"He can't stand gluten-free." Devlin nudged the boy. "Tell her."

A sad, rumpled pout. "I can't stand gluten-free. Please miss. Please may I have a pastry?"

Tara sighed. "And why do you hate gluten-free, little boy?"

"Because my mom can't eat wheat...so there's never anything fun in the house. I never get anything good."

One would think he was dying, the way he wailed. Tara's gaze flicked from the boy to Devlin and back again. "Okay. I will give you a cream puff, but only if you promise not to give him," she thrust a thumb in Devlin's direction, "so much as a bite. Do you promise?"

The boy licked his lips as he nodded. Tara handed over the treasure and nearly laughed out loud at Devlin's dismay as the boy took the treat and scampered over to the tables by the window. He didn't follow, as Tara had expected he would. Instead, he leaned against the pastry case. "So…are you going to the island this weekend?"

"Is that your son?"

It was comical, the way he blanched. "My…no. He's my nephew. My sister is his mom."

"Do you…have any children?"

His grin was crooked. "Don't you think I would have brought my own children in a pathetic ploy to get a cream puff from you, if I had them?"

"Hmm. Probably."

"So, are you going to the island this weekend?"

She meticulously folded a towel. Then fluffed it open and folded it again. "Why do you want to know?"

"I'd…like to see you."

Her heart thundered. Through stiff lips, she said the only thing her brain could conjure. "You said no." He had. He'd refused her offer for meaningless sex outright.

He winced. "I know. Still… I'd like to see you. Maybe drinks at Darby's?"

"A game of pool?" Why her tone was acidic, she had no clue.

"I…" His throat worked. "Sure."

"Well, I won't be there. I have…plans."

"Plans?" There was no need for him to bristle like that, surely. The lilt in his tone made it clear he thought her plans involved another man. Why her heart lifted at that, she had no clue. She'd always hated jealousy in men.

"Yes. Plans."

"What kind of plans?"

"None of your beeswax kind of plans."

He opened his mouth to say something more, but was interrupted when the boy rushed back to the counter, his face smeared with Chantilly cream, and lifted enormous eyes at her and gusted, "That was magnificent! Please miss. May I have another?"

She frowned at him, though it was difficult. He was rather adorable. And far too mischievous to be as polite as he pretended. That Devlin looked terribly put out made her want to grin as well. But she did frown. Because this was an important point. "If I give you another, will you share with this man?"

"No ma'am."

"Not one bite?"

"No way."

"And will you tell him, over and over and over again, how wonderful it was when you're done?"

A nod.

"So good, in fact, it clearly deserves five burps?"

"Um, sure."

"Well okay then. You may have another." She fetched another cream puff and gave it to the boy. "Make sure he realizes what he's missing," she whispered, loudly enough for Devlin to hear.

"Oh, he realizes," he muttered, shooting her a glower. "He realizes just fine."

And somehow, they both knew they weren't talking about the cream puff.

She met her sister the next day at the airport. They saw each other across the booming baggage claim and ran, squealing into each others' arms. It had been so long. Too long.

Stationed overseas for five years, in Germany and Saudi Arabia and finally Kabul, Tina rarely made the trip home. It had been difficult being apart for so long. Growing up—in a military household—they'd done everything together. Moving from pillar to post, Tina had been the only thing in her life that had remained constant.

But now *she'd* changed.

Tara held her back and studied her from tip to toe. They'd always been nearly identical—except now Tina had a close-cropped haircut and shadows in her eyes. And she wore fatigues. Her cheeks were hollow, her figure gaunt. "You've lost weight. Don't they feed you in the Army?"

Tina forced a laugh and copied her perusal. "You've gained weight," she quipped. "See what owning a bakery will do to you?"

"Yeah. Go ahead and mock me. But wait until you taste my cinnamon rolls."

Tina laughed and grabbed her bag as it came around on the carousel. Tara took it from her and nearly dropped it.

"What do you have in here?"

"Bricks."

Their gazes met and they both threw back their heads and laughed.

Damn, it was good having her home.

With Louisa covering the shop, Tara took her sister on a tour of Seattle. Tina hadn't been to the Pacific Northwest since their dad had been stationed at Ft. Lewis when they were in high school, and she'd never really *seen* the town. It was fun experiencing her city through a newbie's eyes. They grazed their way along the bustling corridors of the Pike Place Market, spent a couple hours at the Pacific Science Center, then went down to the wharf to stroll along, peering in the shop windows. They ate clam chowder from a bread bowl at a famous restaurant on the pier. It was late when they got home, but still, they stayed up all night, talking.

Three am was not her friend the next morning. But Tara dragged herself out of bed and into the shower. She was just toweling off when a shrill, piercing scream, followed by a series of growls and grunts echoed through her apartment.

She yanked on her long nightshirt and sprinted for the guest room, flicking on the lights.

Tina rolled around on the bed in a tangle of sheets, bathed in sweat. "No. No. No," she muttered, raising her hand in her sleep to ward off some unseen threat.

"Tina!" When Tara's cry didn't wake her, she approached the bed and shook her sister's shoulder.

Tina sprang up, her expression haunted.

"Tina. It's okay. You had a nightmare."

It took a moment for her sister to find herself, recover. Then she buried her face in her hands and wept.

Tara sat next to her on the bed, wrapped her arm around and held her. "It's okay," she repeated, over and over again. "It's okay."

At long last, Tina stirred. "I'm… I'm so sorry. Did I wake you?"

"No. I was up."

"I thought they'd gone away."

"Gone away?"

Tina sucked in a deep breath and scrubbed at her eyes. "I have nightmares…sometimes."

"About what?"

She tipped her head. "I-I haven't had one for a while. I thought they'd gone away."

"Tina—"

"It's okay, Tara. I'm okay. I need…" She untangled herself from the sheets, padded to her suitcase and pulled out an orange bottle. She cracked it open and measured out two pills, which she tossed back.

"Do you want some water?"

"No. I'm fine. Go back to bed."

Tara barked a humorless laugh. "I'm up for the day."

Tina glanced at the clock on the bedside table. "It's three am."

"I know." Tara grinned. "I'm a baker."

"Oh God, that sucks."

Yeah. It kind of did. "You go back to bed. Do you think you can sleep? Do you want some warm milk?"

A snort. "I'm not a baby. Besides, these will help." She shook the bottle like a maraca.

Tara frowned. She didn't like the idea of her sister relying on pills to sleep. "You—"

"I'm fine." Tina's tone was resolute. "I'll be fine."

But she wasn't fine. She had a nightmare the next night and the night after that as well, bellowing loud enough to wake the neighborhood.

Tara didn't understand her sister's night terrors. Her life had been easy and fun, filled with Chantilly cream and puff pastries. Tina had taken another path, enlisting in the military and serving in three overseas tours. Tara couldn't bear to think what had happened over there to cause this reaction. She did what she could to soothe away the panic, and distract her sister from painful memories.

A tour of the town and a birthday celebration wasn't much—but it was all she had to offer.

For the first time in her life, Tara felt helpless. Utterly helpless.

CHAPTER THIRTEEN

"What do you mean we have to wait two hours? We have a reservation."

Devlin froze at the familiar voice, one that sent prickles along his spine as he wove through the crowded restaurant back to his table. Through the chattering throng, the laughter, the clink of silverware, her voice called to him like a beacon. He scanned the room with a sharp gaze...and saw her. There at the podium, talking to the pompous maître d'.

His knees locked. Damn, she was gorgeous. She wore a short flippy skirt and make up and—his breath seized at this—her hair was down. It flowed over her shoulders like a silky river.

He looked at the man next to her, a hipster with thick rimmed glasses and a shaggy cut. Wearing jeans with a suit jacket. Displeasure snarled in his belly. She was with *him*?

He had no call to be annoyed. He'd said no to her proposition. He'd walked away. She could fuck anybody she wanted.

The fact that he hadn't been able to swallow the regret was his own problem.

Still, it burned to see her with another man...

But then a woman in tight leather pants and matching glasses sidled up to hipster and gave him a kiss. And Devlin's gut unclenched.

As the couple shifted to the side, Devlin noticed Tara's companion. He did a double take. His lips hitched up.

Shit. She had a *twin.*

"But it's our birthday!" Ponytail's voice rose in a warble above the crowd. "We made a reservation."

"I am sorry ma'am," the maître d' said, not sounding sorry at all. "We are very busy tonight."

"It's okay, Tara." The woman next to her crossed her arms and sighed, "We can go somewhere else."

Tara. Her name was Tara.

Resolution rose. He edged closer. So close he could smell her perfume. It clouded his sanity, but he managed to murmur, "You are welcome to sit with us." Tara whipped around and gaped at him. When her eyes met his, he felt like someone had punched him in the gut.

He'd forgotten. Completely forgotten how damn gorgeous she was.

Or maybe he hadn't.

Time hung as their gazes clung. His pulse thudded into the silence as he waited for her to respond.

When she shook her head, his heart plummeted. "We couldn't."

"Don't be silly. We were just seated." He motioned to the maître d' who leapt into action, grabbing two menus.

"Of course Mr. Fox. Right away Mr. Fox."

Being a heartless bastard reviewer had its perks at times.

Devlin took Tara's arm to guide her to his table but she hesitated. He sent her an inquisitive look.

She glanced around the dining room. Her perusal landed on a woman sitting alone at a table by the fireplace. "We wouldn't want to intrude…"

He nearly laughed out loud. She thought he was on a date. *Good.* "It's no intrusion. Really."

She blew out a sigh and frowned at her sister, who shrugged and whispered, "I am kind of hungry." When she added, *sotto voce*, "And he is kind of cute," Devlin couldn't hold back his grin.

"Come along…*Tara.*"

Ooh. That earned him a glare. He didn't mind. He didn't mind at all.

It was about time her name passed his lips.

The maître d' swept up to their table and laid down the menus with a flourish, then snapped his fingers, and a company of servers brought over two extra chairs and place settings. Devlin allowed the maître d' to seat Tara's sister, but he made it a point to hold Tara's chair. It was a chance to be close to her. And he needed to be close to her.

Naturally, she scowled at him.

He leaned in as she sat and whispered into her hair, "It's good to see you again." She frowned at that too.

And it was good to see her again. He hadn't realized how gloomy his mood had been until he'd heard her voice…and the shadows had lifted.

He settled into his seat at her side and nodded to his brother. "This is Charlie. Charlie, meet Tara and…"

"Tina." Tina reached out a hand. Charlie stared at it for a moment, as though he'd forgotten what he was supposed to do, but then slowly lifted his own. He froze as their palms touched. It appeared he did not want to let her go. His lips worked.

"I… ah…" Odd. Charlie usually had a silver tongue when it came to women.

When it appeared Charlie was not going to let her go, Tina pulled her hand away and settled her napkin in her lap, shooting a smile at Devlin. "And who are you? Since Tara doesn't seem inclined to introduce us?"

"I'm—"

"He's Devlin Fox." Tara crossed her arms over her chest and put out a lip. "He gave my bakery a bad review."

"It was not a—"

Tina snorted. "Well, that was stupid."

"It was not a bad review."

Tina shot him a toothy smile. "Tara holds a grudge." She snagged a dinner roll, broke it open and slathered it with butter.

"It wasn't a bad review."

"*Three burps.*"

Charlie gasped with more melodrama than was precisely necessary. In fact, no melodrama was precisely necessary. Devlin glowered, at which his brother grinned. "Why would you give such a beautiful woman only three burps?" *Really, Charlie?* And in that tone of voice? As though he were *seducing* her? And come to think of it, Devlin didn't care for the way his brother was ogling his…his *whatever.*

She wasn't his girlfriend, for God's sake. And she wasn't his lover.

Not technically. She was—

"I didn't know she was beautiful when I wrote the review—" He caught himself and added. "And three burps is *not* a bad review."

Tina clucked her tongue as she opened her menu. "Well, good luck with that."

Charlie fixed Tara with a flirtatious look. "Well, *I* would never give you a bad review."

Devlin tried not to bristle. He needed to complete his review for this restaurant, but why on earth had he brought his brother with him? He should have left the bastard at home with a jar of peanut butter and a spoon.

"Thank you Charlie." Tara patted his hand. "I appreciate that."

"So," Devlin gusted. To distract them, perhaps. "What's everyone going to have?"

Tina slapped the menu closed. "The Shrimp Scampi, I think. How about you?"

"Salmon," Devlin and Tara responded at the same time. Why she had to glare at him about that, he had no clue. It wasn't his fault they had the same taste in fish.

"I'm getting oysters," Charlie said with a waggle of his brows. Honestly, if he didn't quit ogling Tara, Devlin was going to punch him in the gut.

And then he saw it. The flicker in his brother's eye. The quick glance at Tina. And the rise of his blush. And Devlin realized…it wasn't Tara Charlie was interested in. Relief flooded him.

He didn't know why he was so comforted by this knowledge. He had no hold on Tara. No claim to her whatsoever.

He ignored the prickles on his nape at the thought.

The server came to take their orders and the conversation settled into a predictable polite pattern. No talk of burps or grudges. No salacious leers. Tara chatted about her bakery—thankfully without a mention of gluten-free anything—and Tina mentioned that she was visiting for a few weeks. She launched into an entertaining monologue about the sights they'd seen in the past week. It was all very pleasant.

Until Tina turned to Charlie and eyed his wheelchair with a gimlet gaze. "So," she said. "What happened to you?"

Silence descended over the table and Devlin's heart stopped. Froze right there in his chest. He knew he couldn't protect his brother from every wound, but he did try. He just hadn't expected this. Here. Now. And so bluntly.

How mortifying would it be to have a beautiful woman blatantly point out that you were no longer a man?

Charlie's lashes flickered. His Adam's apple worked. But he fixed a tight smile on his face. "IED." Yeah. The bomb had blown a hole in his half-track. Wedged a piece of metal in his spine. He'd been the lucky one.

Devlin opened his mouth to change the topic to something less awkward, but before he could, Tina spoke. "Ah," she said. "That sucks."

"It does indeed."

She tapped the tablecloth with a slender finger. "So, where were you stationed?"

To Devlin's astonishment, his brother shifted toward Tina...as though he wanted to talk about this. "Kandahar."

Tina nodded. Lifted her glass. "Kabul."

"Really?"

"Two years."

"Really?" Charlie looked her up and down. His surprise made it clear he would not have pegged her for a soldier. Neither would Devlin. She was as diminutive and delicate as Tara. Maybe more so. Her short-cut hair and hollowed cheeks made her appear more elfin, even more fragile than her sister. "What's your designation?"

"Med corps."

Charlie whistled through his teeth. "I bet you've seen some things."

"No shit."

The two pattered on, chatting about assignments they'd had, bases they'd both visited, and a bar in Stuttgart they both knew far too well. When they discovered they had mutual friends, any hope of a four-way conversation fled.

Devlin could hardly be offended. He hadn't seen his brother this animated in...too long. He glanced at Tara to catch her gazing at him. Their eyes met and she tried to cover her flush with a little shrug, but it didn't work.

He scooted his chair closer to hers. "I didn't know you had a twin sister," he murmured.

"I didn't know you had a twin brother."

Silence surrounded them. He broke it. "There's a lot you don't know about me."

"There's a lot you don't know about me."

"I'd like to learn." He didn't intend for the words to slip out. They just did. But that was okay. He liked the way her nostrils flared when she caught them. "I meant what I said earlier."

"What was it you said?" She tapped her lip as though trying to remember.

"I missed you...*Tara*." He whispered her name. She shivered. He liked that too.

She affected a blasé shrug. "It's only been a few days."

Since they'd talked, yes. Since they'd touched...far too long. "It's been nearly two weeks. I'm aching."

Her snort surprised him.

"What?"

"Seriously?" She glanced at her sister—who was completely engaged in a conversation with Charlie about mess hall food—and leaned closer to hiss, "You had your chance. You said no."

"Maybe I should have said yes."

The air around them sizzled and crackled.

"Maybe you should have."

He forced a smile. "Do you really hold a grudge?"

"Yes."

"For, ah, how long?"

"Forever." His belly plunged. But when her lips tweaked in a tantalizing offering, something else rose. "But you could...work it off."

"Work it off?"

"Mmm hmm."

If her scorching perusal was any indication, he might enjoy *working it off*. He leaned closer. "Do your worst," he said in a low thrum. "I dare you."

CHAPTER FOURTEEN

Tara's heart stuttered.

Was that a dare?

A serious dare?

Judging from the look in his eye, it was.

She'd been stunned to hear his voice in the crowded restaurant, because she'd been thinking about him. For a second, she'd assumed it was her imagination going crazy, but then she'd turned around and there he was. Standing beside her. So tall and broad and yummy.

It wasn't fair for a man to be so beautiful.

And there were two of them. He had a brother.

She glanced at Tina and Charlie, who had their heads together, laughing about some crazy thing a friend had done. While Charlie shared Devlin's features, almost to a T, his brother had rougher edges. Scars.

But his scars didn't make him less striking. They gave his face a deeper character. Judging from Tina's reaction to him, Charlie's life experience made him even more attractive.

When the waiter came to take their plates and ask hopefully if they'd saved room for dessert, Charlie and Tina emerged from their cocoon. "No dessert for us," Charlie said, tossing his napkin onto the table. "Tina and I are going out dancing."

Devlin gaped at his brother. "D-dancing?" His gaze flicked down to the wheelchair.

Charlie leaned forward, his chin jutting stubbornly. "Dancing. I know a place."

"How can you know a place for dancing?" Devlin must have realized how patronizing he sounded, because he grimaced.

Fortunately, Charlie didn't appear offended. "Because I get out," he quipped. "In fact, *I* have a life. There's a club down the street that has great live music." He turned to Tara and offered an impish grin. "Come with us?"

"I…" She hesitated, but then she noticed Tina's hopeful-puppy expression. "Of course."

Tara allowed Devlin to pick up the tab for dinner because he insisted and, after all, he had agreed to work off his debt to her. Besides, he said he could write it off. But it chafed. It made this interaction feel too much like a date.

She didn't want to date him. She didn't want to date anyone.

But she did want to fuck him.

So as they made their way out of the restaurant into the balmy summer Seattle night, strolling down the street toward the club Charlie knew, and his fingers twined with hers, she didn't pull away.

In an unspoken accord, they both fell back, letting Charlie and Tina lead the way. The two were chatting like magpies, completely enraptured. Charlie's absorption when he looked up at her, as he pushed his wheelchair forward, was telling. As was her responding interest.

"We may have started something there," Devlin murmured into her ear.

She shivered as his warm breath skated over her cheek. "Hmm. They have a lot in common."

"They do. But they like each other too. A lot, it appears."

She peeked at him. A mistake. His blue eyes held a warmth that sent an electric charge through her. Her brain sizzled and popped. Which was probably why she opened her mouth and said, "Maybe it's a genetic attraction."

"Genetic attraction?"

Heat rose on her cheeks. She turned away so he wouldn't notice, but she suspected, from his chuckle, that he did. "We are all twins."

"Are you saying you're attracted to me too, Ponytail?"

She tried to untangle their fingers, but he tugged her closer.

"Are you?" A whisper.

"You know I am." Okay. She probably didn't need to snarl, but he was pushing this a little too far. Declarations were not her thing. Not by a long shot. "But I've been attracted to lots of guys before."

"Hmm." Clearly he did not appreciate this tidbit. "And how did that work out?"

She sent him a reptilian grin. "Dismally."

"Okay." He blew out a sigh and stopped. He still had a hold of her hand so, perforce, she stopped with him. "Where does that put us?"

Tara glanced down the street. Tina and Charlie had continued on, in a world of their own, oblivious they'd lost their companions. Devlin set a finger on her chin and turned her attention back to him. The warmth of his touch irritated her.

This guy could set a fire with a minute caress.

"Us?" She deliberately didn't answer, lobbing the conversational ball back into his court.

"Us." His brow darkened with resolve. And hell, he lobbed it right back. "You're attracted to me and I'm attracted to you. We are attracted to each other. So…where do we go from here?"

"Fuck buddies."

Did she imagine his features tightened at that? "Fuck buddies."

"You did say you wanted to work off your karmic debt to me."

He studied her for a long while. "I, ah, assumed you were joking about that."

She had been. Kind of. But the fact of the matter was, the gambit served a great purpose. If he thought he was expunging his guilt over that crappy review and softening her epic grudge against him, he wouldn't assume what they had was anything other than casual sex. He wouldn't go into caveman relationship mode. She hated caveman relationship mode. She firmed her chin. "Take it or leave it, Devlin."

His response was immediate. He flashed a tight smile, one that didn't reach his eyes, and clipped, "Take it."

"Fine."

"Fine."

"Good."

"Good."

They stared at each other for a long charged moment. The tension around them sizzled and spat. Tara had no idea why there was any tension at all. This was what they both wanted. This was certainly what she *needed*.

Clearly, all the tension was coming from him. Indeed, his muscles were bunched, his shoulders set. His chin—that lovely, delicious chin—was tight. A muscle flexed in his cheek, as though he were grinding his teeth. But it was the look in his eyes that scored her, haunted her.

Surely that wasn't longing?

"Yoo hoo!" A warble echoed down the moonlit street. Tara glanced at Tina and Charlie, who had reached the club. Her sister waved wildly. "Are you joining us?" she called.

"Shall we?" Devlin asked, offering her his arm.

"Yes," she responded. But they both knew they weren't talking about heading for the club. Again, they were talking about something else altogether.

The Pit Stop was a funky little bar with tables and booths surrounding an open dance floor. A fiddler's band played on the small stage at the far end. It wasn't the kind of music Devlin gravitated to, being more of a rock and roll kind of guy, but he liked it a lot.

The place was humming on a Saturday night, but it wasn't hard finding a table near the floor. In fact, a couple of soldiers in uniform waved Charlie over when they saw him roll down the ramp into the establishment. After a short conversation, they vacated their table for them, heading to perch at the bar instead.

"That was nice of them," Tina said, taking her seat.

Charlie winked. "They're friends. They probably think we're on a date and want to give me an advantage."

Devlin didn't miss Tina's blush. Couldn't miss it. It was practically neon. He also didn't miss her frown when the waitress sidled up to his brother and gave him a sultry wink. "Hey, Charliebear."

"Hey Monica."

She set a bowl of peanuts and pretzels on the table. "What can I get you to drink? The usual?"

The usual?

"Yep. And what do you guys want? Beer?" He turned to Tina. "Wine?"

They all rattled off their beverage preferences, but Devlin was in something of a daze. When the waitress left, and Tina and Tara skipped off to the bathroom, as women were wont to do, in herds, he leaned over to his brother. "Do you come here often?"

Charlie barked a laugh. "Is that a pick up line?"

Devlin smacked him. "Be serious. Do you?"

"Occasionally."

"Occasionally enough that the waitress knows you name…and your drink?"

Charlie shrugged. "I like it here. The music is great."

A woman in a slinky dress passed by and blew a kiss. Charlie sketched a salute. Devlin gaped at him.

Holy crap. Despite his disability, his brother did have a life.

The fiddlers kicked into another song and Charlie kept time by tapping his fingers on the table. He looked over his shoulder toward the bathrooms. Apparently Tina had been away from his side for too long.

"Are you serious about dancing?" Devlin tried not to glance at the chair and failed. The thought of Charlie spinning on the dance floor—being stared at by strangers—mortified him.

"I am serious. I love dancing." Charlie's eyes glimmered. He leaned closer. "Brother, sometimes you've got to work with what you've got."

A flutter of movement snagged Devlin's attention. Tara. She and her sister wound their way back to the table, attracting the attention of nearly every man in the bar. She was gorgeous. They both were.

Sometimes you've got to work with what you've got.

And what did he have? A powerful need for a woman. A woman who was attracted to him, but probably nothing more. Was that enough to work with?

"And what if you don't have enough?"

Charlie followed his gaze and clapped Devlin on the shoulder. "You always have enough," he said. "Sometimes you just have to get creative with it."

Resolve formed in Devlin's gut. Yeah, maybe all he had with her was some casual attraction, a fleeting fuckery…for now. But if he was determined, and if he worked what he had very hard, maybe someday it could be more.

But he would have to step cautiously with her. Let their…whatever it was sink slowly into a relationship. This he knew, understood, on an instinctual level. If he pushed too hard or moved too fast, he could lose her.

She wanted casual? He'd give her casual. And hope she didn't just take what she wanted and then waltz away. Sure, it was a risky strategy—one might even call it a dare—but what choice did he have?

And maybe, if he was very lucky, he'd keep her long enough. Long enough for her to change her mind about him. About them. He not only wanted something beyond casual. He *needed* it.

As soon as the ladies returned to the table, Charlie took Tina out "for a spin" on the dance floor, maneuvering his chair through the crowd like a pro. And contrary to Devlin's expectations, the patrons of the bar did not stare at him or laugh or talk about him behind his back. They cheered him on.

It was a huge relief.

Devlin shifted his attention to Tara, sitting next to him, watching the couples twirl on the floor. God she was beautiful. Her dark eyes, her silky hair, the cut of her cheek. Her warmth. He wanted her.

Oh, he had wanted her all night. Before that. Always.

But this was a deeper kind of want. His resolve swelled.

The band started a new song, a slower one.

Devlin ginned. *Perfect.*

"Shall we dance?"

Her gaze snapped to his. Surprise flared on her delicate features. Really? Had she not expected this?

"I...ah. I'm not much of a dancer." She glanced back out at the floor.

He took her hand and stood. "It's easy," he said with a wink. "All you have to do is hold on."

And she better hold on. He was taking her for a ride she would never forget.

CHAPTER FIFTEEN

Lord, he smelled good. That was the only thought in Tara's head as she followed Devlin out onto the dance floor. She trailed in his wake, suffused by the scent of his cologne. But it wasn't his cologne…it was *him*.

When he turned and pulled her into his arms—sealing them together, probably too close, but not nearly close enough—all thoughts flew from her head. A memory, a visceral memory, engulfed her. The two of them, entwined.

"I like this music." His voice rumbled through her as they moved to the beat.

"Hmm. Me too." Was that his hand skating over her back? It sent shivers up and down her spine.

"It's nice." He traced her nape and her pulse hitched.

"Mmm."

He led her in a spin that made her dizzy. Or maybe that was the brush of his groin against hers. The kiss of his hard arousal. The fact that he was hot for her, here, now, amidst a crowd of strangers, excited her.

Inspired her.

He had agreed to her terms. She should be thrilled. She was thrilled. But a part of her was incensed that he had.

A part of her wanted to punish him for that.

They took a few more steps and she returned the favor, rubbing herself against him like a cat on a tuna can. At the same time, she scored her nails along his nape. She loved his guttural groan. It was only a breath, and only in her ear, but it stated—as though he had crowed it aloud—he was completely focused on her every move.

"Tara…"

She peeped up at him. "Yes, Devlin?" A purr.

"Are you teasing me?"

"Who, me?" The batted lashes were probably not necessary. But she liked that the two of them were moving from the earlier awkwardness into roles she understood. She hadn't liked the intensity, the crackling sentiment that had risen up between them tonight. Their relationship had always been casual, playful. She was comfortable there—

Her heart froze as she realized what she'd just thought. Their *relationship*?

They didn't have a relationship.

They had a series of meaningless—although very satisfying—trysts. Trysts did not a relationship make.

Aggravated with herself at the lapse, she pressed into him again, determined to prove, once and for all, that was all this was. She was gratified that he responded. Exactly as he should.

With lust.

He spun her to the edge of the crowd, where the shadows lingered, and pressed her up against the wall. The scrape of his teeth against the tender flesh of her neck made her knees wobble.

"Are you teasing me?" Again, a hushed whisper, but with a band of steel.

In response, she skated her hand over his silky shirt, down the broad muscles of his back, and around front, to wedge between them. "Hmm?"

"Tara…"

She cupped him. He was hard. Engorged. She could feel his pulse thrumming there, in tandem with the ticking vein on his brow. She went up on her tiptoes and nibbled at the underside of his chin, then made her way along the line of his jaw to suck the little spot below his ear, all the while, stroking his heavy cock between their bodies.

He hissed out a harsh breath and pressed them closer together, trapping her hand. "I'm warning you."

She tipped back her head and shot him a grin. "Are you?" His hot gaze blazed into her. "What are you going to do? Teach me a lesson? Here? In public?" This she offered in a pouty tone as she raked her nails over his chest. When she hit his nipples, his entire body clenched.

He flicked a quick glance over his shoulder and around the room and then, without a word, took her arm and yanked her into the hallway leading to the bathrooms.

"Devlin!" she squealed, "I was kidding!"

But he, apparently, was not.

Holy Hannah. That she could inflame him so, with a couple whispers, a caress here or there… Well, it inflamed her too.

He made his way down the empty hall, opening and closing doors. The bathrooms he passed by completely. But then he found a room, way at the back of the hall, a storage room filled with brooms and buckets and cases of toilet paper, and yanked her inside.

"Devlin…"

"Hush."

He silenced her with a kiss, a wild hot, scorching kiss. It was brain numbing, but somewhere in the vast reaches of time and space, she recognized the sound of the lock clicking shut.

He backed her up against the door, fisted his fingers in her hair and held her still as he ravaged her mouth.

He played her, played her like the members of the band played their fiddles. Soft and hard, fast and furious, stretching her nerves and scraping her sanity.

Though he was much taller than she, he insinuated his legs between hers and edged them apart, then bent and pressed his hard cock against her sensitive clit. And rubbed.

She nearly fainted from the ribbons of pleasure wrapping around her, tightening her. Binding her in delight. Her body ached, her nipples pebbled, her pussy wept.

Lord, she wanted him. Needed this.

Craved it.

"Yes, yes."

His response was a grunt. A shift. He skimmed one hand down her flank, pausing to toy with her nipple. Only when he had her shaking did he continue to the hem of her skirt. Teasing fingers danced their way back up, beneath the fabric.

He found her center—how could he not, it was hot and wet and swollen—and traced her gently over her panties.

Then he slipped beneath the band.

The touch of his fingertip on her throbbing clitoris nearly did her in. Hard and tight and aching, it screamed for more. He slipped deeper.

"Devlin—"

"Hush."

His tongue played with her lips, teasing at first, and then he thrust it in. At the same moment, he plunged his fingers deep inside her, stroking her, tormenting her, filling her.

She threw back her head and made a feral sound.

"Hush. We don't want to get caught."

Her pulse launched into overdrive. *They were in public.* She'd nearly forgotten. Hell, she *had* forgotten. It horrified her. And excited her.

The conflicting emotions paralyzed her.

Naturally, he took advantage, continuing, deepening his exploration. She came a little when he thrust in another finger, then came a lot when he added yet another, sinking deep and nudging her here and there and then…*yes, yes, yes.* "Right there. Yes."

"You're so wet." A growl in her ear.

"I'm wet for you."

A snarl. "And so fucking hot."

"I'm hot for you."

He pulled back and glared at her. Perhaps it wasn't a glare, but it was intense and fierce and angry. "Are you? Are you hot for me?"

"You know I am."

"What do you want?" She loved his tone, how clipped and snarly it was.

"You, baby. I want you."

"Who?" A bark.

"What?" He stopped moving inside her and she wiggled a little, to remind him of his task.

"Who do you want?"

"You." She reached for his cock again—to motivate him—but he pressed it against her leg, so she couldn't reach it. She frowned at him.

"Say my name."

Ah. "Devlin. I want you, Devlin. I want you to fuck me."

He did something inside her, something she'd never felt before, and a curtain of heat descended, consuming her face, her neck, her breasts, her belly and finally, her womb. She seized. "Oh. Oh. Oh."

Rapture.

He continued to play her, to keep her orgasm alive, as he unzipped his pants and pulled out his cock. She was possessed of the urge to sink to her knees, to pull him into her mouth and suck him dry, but he did not allow it.

Instead, he slipped on a condom, giving her a dark, determined glance, then wound her loose hair around his fist and turned her, angled her, so she was standing before him. And then he bent her over.

"Spread your legs."

She did so, too addlepated to think about the sopping panties she still wore.

He had not forgotten them.

He slipped his fingers into the crotch and ripped them off in one harsh yank. She didn't even have the wherewithal to protest because without delay, he took her.

His cock felt good, slipping into her folds. So large and full. Warm. Thrumming. He thrust deep, taking her all the way.

The hovering orgasm pinged again and she clenched at him.

He sucked in a breath. "Is this what you want? Is this why you were teasing me tonight?" Another thrust.

"Yes. Yes." She might have been answering his question, or not. It hardly mattered. She suspected it had been a rhetorical question anyway.

"God, baby." He anchored his grip on her hips and held her steady, yanking out and plunging deep again. Each lunge sent slivers of delight dancing along every nerve. "So tight. So deep."

The sound of flesh slapping flesh mingled with their grunts and groans, the music thrumming through the amplifiers a mere wraith in the background. Everything was there, in that place they connected. As though all existence shrank down to that one magnificent merging.

She spread her legs further and pushed back into him, flattening herself against him as he took her from behind. With each lunge, his balls slapped against her raw clit. As his pace increased, tightened, became more frantic, the sensation intensified, overtook her.

She didn't even bother holding back. She gave her release full rein. Her body seized, shook. Her pulse raced. A wet heat flooded her. Sensation exploded, taking her along on a spinning journey, a panoply of dancing colors and mindless joy.

His thrusts devolved into short, hard jerks and then to nothing but shudders. But each movement beset her with a wash of gentle bliss, like a receding wave, leisurely lapping the shore.

Still buried deep, he held her as they recovered.

Why was it he always left her gasping for breath? Brainless and boneless and wanting more?

She sighed and relaxed against him.

"Good?" He murmured, kissing her neck and running a hand down her body.

"Hmm." So good. So incredibly fucking good.

He slipped beneath her skirt again and stroked her sensitive clit. She lurched as another wave scudded her senses and they separated. She forced a chuckle. "Sorry," she said, not meeting his eye. It wouldn't do for him to know how deeply that had affected her. In fact, *she* didn't even want to face it. "Where are my panties?"

He looked around, squinting against the murk of a room lit by nothing more than the flickering beacon of the smoke alarm. "Here they are." He picked them up and held them out to her.

She couldn't hold back a snort.

"What?"

"You shredded them." She dangled them between her fingers. Good God. They were destroyed. "Do you have any idea how much these cost?"

He shot her a crooked grin as he pulled up his pants. "Sorry?"

She frowned. "Not only did you drag me back into a storage closet filled with nasty mops—"

"They are hardly nasty at all."

"And fuck me like a two penny whore—"

"I would definitely have paid more."

"You shredded my underwear. Shredded them."

"I'll buy you new ones." His expression indicated he might enjoy the prospect.

She smacked him with them and broke out in a laugh when he grabbed them and brought them to his nose, taking a big gusty whiff. "Devlin Fox!"

Her admonishment had no effect. In fact he waggled his brows, murmured, "Yummy," and tucked her bedraggled panties into his pocket.

"What do you think you're doing?"

His lips curved. "Keeping them."

"For what?"

He suddenly sobered. His gaze was scorching. "For later."

She sighed. "What do you need them for…later?"

He leaned in and kissed her. In the hazy green glow of the smoke alarm, she couldn't help but notice the harsh, hungry lines of his face. "Because, darling, now we have to go out there and chit chat and act as though we didn't just fuck like animals in this broom closet. And for the rest of the night, I have to deal with the knowledge that you aren't wearing any panties."

She shook her head. "But what does that—"

Realization dawned.

Unbidden, her attention drifted down to his pants, to the pocket in which he'd stuffed her panties. A soft little bulge.

And right next to it…a hard one.

CHAPTER SIXTEEN

As he escorted Tara back to the table, Devlin was a little wobbly. His knees were weak, his pulse was thrumming and—inconceivably—he was hard again. Hard for her.

After that. After the most amazing, mind-blowing, incredible closet sex he'd ever had. Technically, it was the only closet sex he'd ever had, but still. By all laws of nature, he should be limp as a wet noodle for a week. But he wasn't.

He wanted her again.

Thankfully, the bar was murky and crowded and no one seemed to notice his hard on. He scanned the room to make sure no one was staring at them, but the other patrons in the bar were all oblivious.

Charlie and Tina were oblivious as well. To everything but each other. As he and Tara approached the table, the two had their heads together in deep conversation, not even emerging when he and Tara took their seats.

He glanced at her. Was he the only one who could see the sheen of dew on her cheeks? The glint in her eye? The slight upward tilt of her lips? Was he the only one who could see how freshly-fucked she looked?

God, he hoped so.

He had no idea how much noise they'd made and was thankful no one had come to investigate. That would have been awkward.

But even if they'd been caught, he would probably do it again. And again. Any chance he got.

Half of his exhilaration came from the residual effects of that mind-bending fuck. The other half stemmed from the fact that he'd had her again. He'd so missed her touch, her scent. Her presence.

He wasn't crazy about their fuck buddies agreement, but at least it was something. And like Charlie said, at least something was something. It was a place to *start*.

He took her hand and she allowed it, though she drew their laced fingers beneath the table to rest on his thigh. He liked that, holding hands with her under the table…until her thumb reached out to skim over his slacks.

Hell. Was she teasing him? Again? He sent her a glower, but there was little heat in it. How could there be? He had little heat left to give. She'd taken it all.

She smiled in return and offered a saucy wink.

And something inside him tipped to the side. It might have been the universe.

It was a strange place and time to realize something so potent— with the fiddlers playing in the background and the glasses clinking at the bar and Charlie and Tina nattering on—but maybe it simply happened when it did. But all of a sudden, Devlin realized why he had ached for her so bad. Why he had missed her so much. Why being with her again had flooded him with elation. Why he was willing to do anything, offer everything, to be with her.

Yeah. He loved her. Loved her with a capital L.

Loved her smile, loved her laugh. Loved her frown and her growls. Loved her face. Her hair, her body, her scent. Loved her heart and mind and soul.

The realization scared him to death…and excited him beyond belief.

The buzzing noise in the back of his head turned out to be Charlie and Tina discussing ideas for an outing. Since Tina was leaving soon, Charlie wanted to show her around the area tomorrow.

His brother glanced across the table. "You two are welcome to come along," he said, clearly as an afterthought.

"Oh, you must." Tina turned to her sister. "We don't have much time together as it is. I don't want to miss a whole day."

"What do you have planned?" Tara asked, munching on a peanut from the bowl.

Charlie beamed. "First we're going hiking." Devlin grimaced. He was not much of a hiker. "And then we're going to Snoqualmie Falls."

"How can we... I mean..." He tried very hard not to look at Charlie's chair. "Hiking?"

"Both the Burke-Gilman Trail and the Sammamish River Trail are wheelchair accessible," Charlie said, shooting Devlin a teasing scowl. Or maybe not so teasing. "This is the twenty-first century, after all."

"Mmm." Tara murmured. "The Locks to Lakes Corridor."

"Exactly. It'll be fun." Charlie gored Devlin with a gimlet gaze. "Are you in?"

Devlin tried to hide his pout. He wanted to spend time with Tara, but walking for fun was, well, not fun. He'd never quite understood his brother's passion for the outdoors.

But he'd attended a BDSM party for her—with the sole purpose of being near her once again. And that had paid off. Maybe he should give it a try.

"Well? Are you?"

"I suppose," he grumbled, shifting in his seat. Tara's grin caught his attention.

It was an exceedingly evil grin.

To his surprise, he thoroughly enjoyed the day. For one thing, Tara was there, and in a playful mood. For another, he got a glimpse of the other side of his brother. One he'd never seen before.

A man who was capable and determined—stubborn, even. A man who could overcome any obstacle.

The difference for Charlie was that the obstacles were more plentiful. A raised curb, for example. Devlin stepped over it without a thought. For Charlie, it required a little maneuvering. But he could do it. He could do anything.

With a wash of mortification, Devlin realized how wrong he'd been to underestimate his brother. He'd known Charlie his whole life. He should have known better.

Maybe it was time for Devlin to reevaluate his thinking. Maybe Charlie wasn't a helpless cripple after all. Maybe the ability to stand on your own two feet wasn't what defined a person after all.

Life tossed all kinds of IEDs into a man's path. The measure of his mettle was how he dealt with them.

Charlie, it appeared, embraced the adventure, despite the difficulties. When they came to the first slight slope, he not only released his hold on his wheels, he pushed harder, flying down the grade with Tina jogging by his side. They both laughed. In those trills, Devlin heard it. The sheer joy of being alive.

And he realized, he'd missed it. The big picture.

In Charlie's mind he wasn't *disabled*. He was *blessed*. He was a survivor. With everything he'd seen and done, with everything he'd been through, being alive was a gift. A treasure. No matter the circumstances.

It was humbling. And heartening.

Tara sidled up to him and hooked her arm in his as they strolled along the paved path, passed by runners and bicyclists and dog walkers. Devlin had had no idea so many people liked to be *outside*. It was kind of surprising.

"What are you thinking?" she asked.

"Hmm?"

"You look pensive. Are you composing an amusing review of last night's dinner?"

He blinked in surprise. Hell. He hadn't even thought about last night's dinner. The service had been a trifle sycophantic, but not execrable. The food—well, he couldn't even remember the food. All of his attention had been on her. "No. I need to write it though. What did you think?"

"Me?" A squeak.

"Yeah." He smiled down at her, loving the lines of her face. He wanted to trace her cheek, but thought better of it. She'd probably think that too loverly. "What were your impressions of the meal?"

She scrunched up her nose—adorable—and nibbled her lip. He tried not to fixate on that. If he swept her in his arms and planted one on her right here in the middle of the trail, that would definitely be too loverly. But God Almighty in Heaven Above. He wanted to.

"The salmon was fishy."

He barked a laugh. "Salmon *is* fishy."

"You know what I mean. *Fishy* fishy. It was probably Atlantic, though it said Coho on the menu."

Wow. He gaped at her. The woman knew her salmon. Come to think of it, there had been an oily aftertaste more prominent in

Atlantic salmon. Yeah. That dish had not been Coho. "And the broccolini?"

"Pretentious."

He untangled their arms and slipped his around her, pulling her close to his side. Where she belonged. He kissed her forehead. "You, my darling, should have been a food critic."

"And I think I broke a tooth on a dinner roll. Oh. Oh. Oh. And the wine was a little vinegary."

"What?" That wine had cost a fortune.

"There was a spot on my spoon, the risotto was soupy and what was with the cologne on the waiter?"

Devlin chuckled. He'd created a monster. Ah well. No matter. He needed the material. "May I quote you?"

She growled a little in her throat. "Don't you dare. I don't want my name on your icky blog."

"It's not an icky blog. It's a very popular blog."

"Still, I don't want that wild-eyed maître d' coming after me because I mentioned he has a duck walk."

"A duck walk?"

"Didn't you notice?"

"Um, no." The maître d' had been the last thing on his mind, once he'd seen her.

She pulled away and demonstrated, tottering from side to side with her knees locked. She glanced back at him and quacked three times in quick succession—purely for illustrative purposes. And, now that she'd mentioned it, the maître d' had waddled. A tad.

But he hadn't quacked.

"Did you like anything about the meal?"

She sobered. "You were there."

Ah. God. His heart swelled. His pulse thrummed. He cast about, looking for a somewhat private spot to steal a kiss. There was nothing but trees and bushes sprinkled along the ribbon of trail. No place at all for a furtive clinch.

Which was probably why he hated the out of doors.

Her lips curled in a soft smile and he decided he didn't care if she thought him too loverly. He didn't care if anyone saw. He didn't care if the world saw.

He swooped her into his arms and kissed her, but good. He kissed her until a speed-walking mommy shuttled past with her speed-walking children and snarled, "Get a room."

And they both laughed. Because it wasn't the first time they'd heard that.

At their next stop, Devlin discovered a definite benefit to outings with Charlie. With a blue placard hung on the rearview mirror, he didn't have to park in the boondocks and walk, as Devlin had so many times before when he'd visited this popular destination. There were plenty of handicap parking spaces right next to the Snoqualmie Falls observation deck.

They had to meander up the switchback of ramps leading to the covered platform overlooking the falls, but it was a fair trade. And though Devlin offered, Tina insisted on pushing Charlie up the steeper slopes. Judging from the wink Charlie sent him, he enjoyed her enthusiasm.

They could hear the thundering rush of the water before they crested the rise, feel the sudden dampness of the air on their skin. They reached the top of the slope and stopped at the chain link fence running along the cliff's edge, and stared.

It was magnificent.

Even if he hadn't seen it before, he would have been stunned to silence.

The sheer power of nature, the rushing tumult of the drop, the rainbows dancing in the mist shrouding the base of the falls. Breathtaking.

"Glorious," Tara whispered at his side. He hooked his arm around her and pulled her close.

"You should see them when all the snowmelt floods the river. The falls cover the entire cliff face and pound into the water below." The last time he'd come here during the melt, the power of the falls had shaken the earth beneath his feet. And the spray had risen to engulf the entire gorge.

"I thought you weren't an outdoorsy guy."

He shrugged. "I'm not. But this is a great place to bring a date for dinner."

He probably imagined the flicker of displeasure. Then again, maybe not.

She pushed away and shoved her hands into her pockets. Her

brow puckered. "Bring a lot of dates here?"

A lot. "A few. There's a great restaurant in the lodge."

"And a hotel." This, she muttered.

Devlin couldn't help but bite back a grin. Dare he hope she was jealous? "True. It's a very nice hotel." He turned his attention back to the water, but was really focused on her, from the corner of his eye. "It's quite romantic. Especially at night."

She snorted.

"They light the falls."

"Do they?"

He stepped closer. "Would you like to see it…sometime?"

Her glance was wary. "Maybe."

"Maybe?"

She nibbled on her lip, again, distracting his attention from the conversation. "How many women have you brought here?"

Oh hell. No.

"A few."

"A few is three."

"Okay. More than three."

"More than five?" She frowned at his nod. "More than ten?" He shrugged. She smacked him. "Damn it Devlin. How many women have you had?"

Charlie rolled by just then, because he was a master of bad timing, and crowed, "Legions."

And all of a sudden, teasing Tara like this wasn't funny anymore at all.

CHAPTER SEVENTEEN

They had a delicious lunch in the restaurant of the lodge perched at the top of the falls. As hard as he tried, Devlin couldn't think of anything to complain about. He chalked that up to the companionship—specifically the fact that Tara was by his side. Conversation flowed naturally, and when they all paused to stare out the window at the falls below, no one minded.

The discussion was eclectic, ranging from Charlie's adventures overseas to Tara's descriptions of some of her more eccentric customers to irate comments Devlin had fielded on his blog. But when the topic turned to Tara and Tina's childhood, his attention was snared.

"How many times did you move?" Charlie asked, picking an onion off his sandwich.

"Nineteen," Tina replied. "Before high school graduation."

"Wow." Devlin glanced at Tara. "That's a lot."

She shrugged. "Typical of the military."

"Oh?" Charlie tipped his head in interest. "Army brats?" At Tina's nod, he asked, "Is that why you joined up?"

Tina took a sip of her iced tea and munched on a fry before she answered. "Yep. I was going for the continuity thing."

Tara snorted. "There's no continuity in a military lifestyle."

"There's nothing but continuity in a military lifestyle."

"Seriously?" She glared her sister down. "You move all the time, have to meet all new people, have to learn a new place... I hated it."

Tina shook her head. "The rules are the same everywhere you go, and everyone understands them. It's not like the civilian world, where you never know what to expect."

"Word."

Tara narrowed her eyes on Charlie, not appreciating his intrusion in their family squabble. "Everything is temporary. Nothing is forever. Not your house. Not your friends or your school or your...anything!"

Tina set her chin. "Family is forever."

Tara gored her sister with a dark frown. "Is it? Tell that to mom." She didn't seem to notice how her sister paled. She continued on. "As soon as you get used to a place, orders come in to move on and you have to *leave*. Leave it all behind, everything you've built, and walk into some new freaking normal. Constant flux. Constant adjustment. I hated it."

"I loved it," Tina offered softly. So softly, it gave Tara pause. Or made her stop ranting, at least. Though, as awkward as that moment had been, it had been illuminating.

Because it helped Devlin see, helped him understand *why*.

Tara's resistance to a relationship didn't stem from his lack as a man. It stemmed from a childhood filled with insecurity and incessant change. He could see her as a young girl, confused, buffeted, trying to cling to something in this world that did not slip away...and failing.

What she wanted, what she needed and craved beyond bearing, was the very thing she kept pushing away. A forever. With a man.

Because she was afraid, she had convinced herself, it wasn't possible to find.

Without thought, he put his arm around her and stroked her shoulder with his thumb. Her brow furrowed, but she didn't protest. In fact, after a moment, she seemed to relax into his caress. So he didn't stop. Didn't ever want to stop.

"Wasn't there anything you liked about our childhood?" Tina asked. Devlin noticed she had ripped her bread to shreds. It mounded in a mutilated pile on her plate.

Tara nibbled her lip. "Well... We did get to travel." To his relief, the tension between the two sisters eased with her response.

"Yes. We did." Tina smiled.

"Where were you stationed?" Charlie asked, before Devlin could form the words.

"We lived in Germany and Japan and Taiwan." Tina ticked the list off on her fingers.

"And Oklahoma," Tara added. "Don't forget Oklahoma."

A laugh. "And Virginia and California…"

"And Washington State." Tara sobered at that and shot her sister a glance. There may have been tears glinting in her beautiful eyes. Yes. Definitely tears. "That was when dad left." This was a whispered addition, but they all heard.

Tina reached across the table and covered Tara's hand with her own. "They were better apart."

"Hmm." Tara blew out a breath and picked up the dessert menu the server had left, in a blatant attempt to end the conversation. "Anyone want to share something?"

A knot formed in Devlin's throat. A knot he couldn't seem to swallow.

He did. He wanted to share something… But he could hardly say *that*, so instead he stroked her back and murmured, "See anything you like?"

Her minxish grin was the Tara he knew, spunky and mischievous and fearless. But the shadows lingered. Upon reflection, he realized they had always been there.

"Well," she gusted. "They do have a peanut butter soufflé…"

"Really?" he murmured into her ear. "Is it creamy or chunky?"

It was a relief when Tina announced she and Charlie were going out that night. Not that Tara didn't enjoy spending time with her sister, but after their exchange over lunch, she felt like they needed a break from each other's company.

Also, it prompted Devlin to turn to her and ask, very sweetly, if she would like to spend the evening with him.

She only dithered for a moment. And then, only because the specter of all his other girlfriends rose in her mind. Hell, she knew he'd been around the block…at least once. What she didn't understand was why it bugged her. But she pushed her disquiet away and accepted.

They all tromped back to Charlie's van and climbed in—she was getting used to the machinations required, with the wheelchair and all. And while Devlin offered to help, Charlie refused, impressing them all, once again, with how stubborn and self-sufficient he was. He swung up into the van then reached down and folded his chair, hefting it neatly into its spot behind the driver's seat.

Conversation was light and cheery as they made the drive back to Seattle. They all marveled at the beauty of the forest surrounding the falls and how such rampant natural beauty was only a short drive from a major metropolis.

Charlie dropped Tara and Devlin at his house and then, with a hug from Tina, those two took off.

As she made her way up the ramp to Devlin's place—which she was dying to see—she tossed him a grin. "So what did you want to do?"

"We could go out for dinner..." The way he trailed off told her he was making the suggestion solely out of deference to her preferences.

"Do we have to?" Yeah. She liked the way his features lit up.

"Or we could stay in. Maybe watch a movie." He unlocked the door and pushed it open, gesturing for her to enter. The entry hall was wide and airy and spotless.

"I'd like that. But..."

He fixed her with a tense gaze. "But what?"

She made a face. "I have to work in the morning. *Early.*"

"Ahh." He turned away. Ostensibly to close the door, but she suspected he wanted to hide his response as well. He'd been doing that a lot lately.

"Why do you say it like that?"

"What?"

"You said 'Ahh.'" She attempted to mimic his tone. "As though you don't believe I really have to work early."

"It is a standard gambit..."

She snorted a laugh and peeked around the corner to survey his living room. Also spotless. And *so* Devlin. Thick leather couches and heavy wood end tables, but lightened with a lush cream Flokati rug. Built-in bookshelves, filled to the gills, flanked the hearth. She stepped closer to examine the painting over the fireplace. A print of *The Wave* by Hokusai. She had one, a smaller one, at home. "It's not a gambit. I *do* have to work early." She grinned. "I am a baker, remember?"

Their gazes tangled. His heated. "You really have to work early?"

"I need to be there at four."

He winced. "Four? In the *morning?* Really?"

"Yup. I get up at three." This had always been a point of contention with previous boyfriends, but Devlin only grinned.

"Well then," he said. "We'd better get started."

And then he stalked across the room, yanked her into his arms and kissed her.

It was heaven, absolute heaven, holding her, kissing her again. Devlin could have done just that all night. But another pressing need arose as their passion ignited. He pulled back and stared down at her beautiful face. She was flushed, dewy. Her lips were parted, damp. An idea, an inspiration, a raw, primal need flared.

"Do you know what I hate?" he asked, his voice catching on his lust.

She tipped her head to the side. "What do you hate?" Was she aware her fingers toyed with the hair at his nape? He doubted it. Didn't care.

"People who welsh on a bet."

She blinked, clearly not expecting him to say that. "Okay. And why do you feel the urge to mention that now? At this very moment?" She tried to pull him back into the kiss, but he resisted.

"Because you *owe* me."

She snorted. "*I* owe *you?*"

He tsked. "Oh, how soon they forget."

"What are you talking about Devlin?" she said on a laugh.

"Come here." He took her hand and led her down the hall and into the kitchen. She watched, arms akimbo, as he riffled in the pantry. But when he pulled out a jar of peanut butter, she got it. Her eyes widened. Her mouth formed an entrancing little *O*. Which inflamed him.

Exactly.

He waggled the jar. "Remember?"

He loved the way her expression changed. From slightly befuddled to intrigued to downright wicked. She took the jar from him and perused the label. "Hmm. Extra chunky." She glanced at him from beneath veiled lashes. "Kinky."

He laughed, but when she pushed him into the chair and barked, "Sit," his amusement faded.

"Here?"

"Where else but the kitchen?" She unscrewed the plastic top and took a whiff. "Mmm. I do love peanut butter. Take off your slacks."

"Are you going to steal them?" he asked through a chortle, but he complied. With alacrity.

"Maybe."

His breath caught in his throat as she knelt between his knees on the hard kitchen floor. Really? He'd been thinking they could do this upstairs on a soft mattress...but who was he to interrupt a woman determined to fulfill a debt of honor? She peeped up at him, licked her lips and rolled his briefs down. His cock sprang free, ready, willing and decidedly eager. His cock loved peanut butter too...apparently.

She took him in her hands, a two-fisted hold, and his sanity skittered. She leaned closer and drew in his scent and moaned. "You smell so good."

Jesus and Jujubes. He shifted impatiently.

She dipped a couple fingers into the jar and scooped out a healthy dollop of peanut butter and—*shit*—rubbed it on the head of his cock. The grating rasp of the peanut chunks made him go cross-eyed. She smoothed the gooey substance along his shaft, rubbing it in with a hellish rhythm.

His balls tightened. His pulse pounded. Burning need seethed. God. He wasn't going to last. He should never have brought this up.

It was nearly a relief when she stopped. Or maybe not.

She sat back on her haunches to survey her handiwork, and he twitched his hips, thrusting a little in her direction. Something mischievous danced in her smile. "This is where I walk away, I think."

His heart plunged. "Don't you dare!" A growl. Feral and hungry. She'd better fucking not walk—

She laughed at his expression and took his cock in her firm grasp once more. "Fortunately," she whispered, "I'm hungry." She kissed the tip, swirled her tongue over the hyper-sensitive surface. Shivers of delight racked him. "And I do love peanut butter..."

If he'd thought she was tormenting him before, he had no idea what torment was. Because now she attacked him with fervor, licking and sucking and lapping with that velvet tongue. Here, there, up the shaft, down around his balls, the underside of his glans...everywhere.

Over and over and over again until he thought he might lose his mind with the pleasure.

He put his hand on the top of her head, wove his fingers in her hair and gently tried to guide her. The result was disaster. She stopped.

She pulled back with a fulminating frown, but he could tell it was an act. At least, he hoped it was. She looked pretty fierce. "Hands to yourself, buster."

"But—"

"Hands to yourself." She arranged his arms at his side and fit his fingers around the back legs of the wooden chair. "There. Hold on to that. And don't let go."

His Adam's apple worked. "Or what?" A whisper. A hope?

"Or I'll really punish you."

Oh yeah. It was an act. She couldn't stop her lips from tweaking, though he could tell she was trying very hard to appear adequately stern.

"Really?"

"Really."

"Wh-hat… H-how…"

"I don't know. Maybe I'll tie you up and tease you for hours." *Oh hell no.* "Or maybe I'll tie you up and leave." *Double hell no.*

"Tara…" She ignored his plea. Was it a plea? Probably.

"You hold on and sit there like a good boy and I will finish you." God, her tone excited him. He didn't know why. Or maybe he did. "But if you let go…I stop. Got it?"

He shouldn't have laughed, but it was a nervous laugh, a *holy-shit-is-this-really-happening* kind of laugh, so it probably didn't count. "Tara…"

"What's the matter, Devlin? Can't you take a dare?"

Oooh. Her words got him right in the gut. Or maybe it was her sultry glance. He firmed his chin. "Okay. I accept your dare."

"Don't you let go."

He wouldn't. Not if it freaking killed him. And it might. "Okay, wench," he said, trying to goad her back to work. "Do your worst."

Maybe he shouldn't have added that last bit. Maybe that goaded her too far, because she did go back to work and man, was she ruthless. But he held on as she worked him, as she stroked and sucked and fondled his rock hard, pounding erection. He held on for dear life.

The abrasion of the little chunks scraped at his nerves, his sanity, and when all the peanut butter was gone, she kept licking and lapping, kept sucking, kept teasing, until he wanted to scream.

Tension built and built within him. Heat, agony, a blistering ache for release. "Tara…"

"Don't bother me," she said. "I'm busy."

"Tara…"

His tone must have reached her, the sheer naked desperation sinking through her absorption. She stilled and peeped up at him, her mouth stretched around his cock.

And fuck.

Fuck fuck fuck.

He couldn't stop the scorching tide, the screaming rush of cum. It exploded from him in agonizing, rapturous jets. One after the other after the other, for eternity.

Despite his blinding bliss, they didn't break eye contact as she took it all, took him. She tightened her suction and urged him on to higher and higher pleasure, moaning around him in a hellish vibration as she tasted him, swallowed him, drank everything he had to give.

CHAPTER EIGHTEEN

Tara sat back and looked up at Devlin. His eyes were closed, his muscles tight. He clung to the chair as though it were a lifeline in a churning sea. An expression of absolute elation and peace lit his striking features. Her heart thudded. She'd done that. She'd pleased him beyond bearing.

And good lord, had that been fun. She hadn't expected she'd enjoy bossing him around quite so much. She enjoyed even more that he'd obeyed.

His eyes opened and he gazed at her. His lips worked.

"Are you okay?" she asked.

In response he released his hold on the chair, threaded his fingers in her hair and dragged her close. And he kissed her. It was hot, hard and feral. She tasted a gratitude that surprised her.

His intensity made her a little uncomfortable. She didn't understand why. She covered her discomfort by reaching down to tug up his briefs. He stood—a little wobbly—and pulled them all the way up, along with his slacks. Then he reached out a hand and helped her to her feet. And into his arms. And he kissed her again.

"Did you enjoy your PBBJ?" she asked when he gave her a chance to breathe.

His chuckle resonated through her. "Is that what the kids are calling it nowadays?"

She grinned. And then kissed him. Because he was too cute to resist.

"Come on," he said, wrapping his arm around her and leading her into the hall.

"Where are we going?" she asked, though she really didn't care. As long as he was there. She didn't bother to examine that thought. Or what it might mean.

"Into the living room. I need to relax." Indeed, he was still shaking a little.

They settled on his soft, leather couch and he pulled her into his arms, tucking her head beneath his chin. And he held her. She liked the warmth of his embrace. His scent rose up to suffuse her. His heart beat against her ear in a rapid tattoo.

She stroked his arm as he rubbed her back and slowly, his heartbeat returned to a less frantic pace.

"I enjoyed that tremendously," he said after a long long while.

"It was fun."

His chest heaved as he barked a laugh.

"What?"

"You're quite the little Domme when you choose to be."

She snorted.

"No, really. When you glared at me and barked, *Sit,* I almost came right then."

She tipped up her head and raked him with a playful scrutiny. "Devlin Fox, I would never have pegged you for a kinky guy."

"I can be." He winked. "Chunky peanut butter…"

She chuckled and leaned her head against him again and the conversation lapsed. But it was a comfortable lapse. He toyed with her hair. Teased her neck. It was nice.

"I've been wondering about something," he said into the breach.

"Hmmm?"

"Why do you think Avery gave us *Switch* at her party?"

Tara's brow knit. She glanced up at him again. "I think it was random."

"Was it?" He smiled. An angelic, beautiful mien. Her attention drifted to his lips. "Does Avery ever do anything random?"

Come to think of it…no. "Never."

"I think she was making a statement to us."

"Aside from matching us up, even though we both insisted we were not together?"

"You insisted. Not me. And yes. Aside from that."

"What do you think she was saying?"

"Typical Avery. She was commenting on the dynamics she saw in us during that pool game."

"She was only there for a few minutes."

"Maybe it was that clear."

She pulled back so she could see him more clearly. She didn't like the way the cool air rushed between them. "What?"

"Our energy. You know how in each relationship, one partner or another is a little more dominant?" He caught her expression and laughed. "Or, in some cases, a lot more dominant."

"Yeah?"

"I think we're evenly matched."

"Do you?" Why his words warmed her, she had no clue. And the fact that he'd just said the "R" word and it didn't cause the little hairs on her neck to rise was a mystery as well.

"You enjoyed my spanking and hell, I sure enjoyed that." He thrust a thumb at the kitchen.

"Did you?"

"Shit, Tara. That was mind-blowing."

She preened a little. "Why thank you sir."

"I think it would be fun to explore this a little."

Her heart hiccupped. "What do you mean? In a dominant submissive kind of way?"

"Not exactly…" He flicked a gaze at her. "Unless you want to—"

"No." Unequivocally. No. It was fun to play around with it, but anything beyond that was too much for her. "So what were you thinking?"

"I kind of like our dares."

She kind of liked that he pulled her back in his arms. Where it was warm. "Oh, do you?"

"Yeah. I think we should dare date."

She had to glance up at him at that. "Dare date?"

"Mmm hmm."

"And what is that, exactly?"

"We dare each other."

"On a *date*?" He knew she didn't want to date.

"Let's call it a sexual interaction." Then, after a moment of thought, he added, "But there may be dinner, or a movie, or something like that included."

"A package deal?"

"Yeah. Something like that. For example, I wouldn't mind taking you to the movies. Nothing popular, nothing first run. Just a movie in a darkened theatre. Deserted, preferably."

His meaning hit her like a ton of bricks. "And what would you dare me to do in that deserted, darkened theatre?" A purr.

His grin sent heat along every nerve. "You'll have to wait and see, baby. "You'll have to wait and see."

Charlie and Tina saw each other every day that week when Tara was at work and every afternoon, Devlin swung by to pick her up for a dare date. He made it a point to get her home by seven, on the dot.

Though she appreciated his punctuality, it began to chafe after a while. Because sometimes, they'd be in the middle of something, something fun, and he'd check his watch and tell her they had to hurry. For the first time in her career, she began to resent the bakery. For the first time in her career, she began think about loosening the reins a little and hiring more help.

Jose loved the idea. He had a cousin with experience who was looking for work. And of course, Louisa was happy for the extra shifts. With business picking up again, she could definitely afford it. She decided to interview Jose's cousin and give him a test run that week with Jose's supervision.

And damn, was it worth the cost. Having time with Devlin, something more leisurely than a few snatched hours here and there, was wonderful. And, as it turned out, he was a devious son of a bitch. Definitely kinky, but in the best possible way.

He inspired her as well. Inspired her to come up with crazier and crazier dares.

They had sex in the movie theatre, of course, and in an elevator, on the ferry and in a bathroom stall of his favorite bar. He dared her to wear stilettos and a short skirt—and *no* underwear—to a Mariner's game and she dared him to visit Bella's sex shop and ask to be fitted for a collar.

The *coup de gras* was when she dared him to get a Brazilian Wax. He did it—which astounded her—but he screamed like a little girl.

It was a wild week. An amazing week. Fun and sexy and exciting and crazy. She didn't want it to ever end. To her surprise, she found she wanted to be with him more and more, and was annoyed when work—or life—pulled her away.

She didn't mind their double dates with Tina and Charlie, because those two were so wrapped up in each other, they didn't pay much attention to what Devlin and Tara were up to. Which was often something naughty.

But Tina was leaving soon. Time with her was precious, so Tara made arrangements to take her sister to the island that weekend, so she could see the retreat Tara loved so much—and maybe meet some of her friends. But to her mortification, when Tina came to the bakery for breakfast Thursday morning, she let slip that she'd already made other plans. She and Charlie had booked an overnight trip to Victoria.

"An overnight? Seriously?" Tara gaped at her sister over the table.

"Yes."

"But you just met."

Tina laughed. "It doesn't matter how long you've known someone, silly. When its right, you know it."

Tara swallowed. "And…it's right?"

"It's very right. Charlie and I have so much in common. I enjoy his sense of humor and his strength. He gets me. I mean…" She flushed. "He *understands*. Really understands. And man, is he a good kisser."

"A good…kisser?" For some reason, she'd never imagined the two of them, well, kissing.

"Hoo mama. I can't wait for this weekend."

It was hard not to put out a lip. "But what about me? This is your last weekend."

Tina tipped her head to the side and gazed at her. "I'll see you again. Soon. I'm…retiring."

"Retiring! You're too young to retire."

She chuckled. "Not in military terms. I think I've had enough deployments."

"I thought you loved it."

"I do. But… Well, this visit helped me see that there was something missing from my life."

"Charlie?" Tara swallowed the lump in her throat.

Tina's lashes fluttered. "Maybe. I've always been a career soldier—to the exclusion of all else. But it's time I paid attention to other aspects of my life. It's time I settled down. And Tara... Charlie proposed."

Tara gaped at her. "But you just met him!"

"Would you be so bummed if I moved here?"

"Bummed? Hell no! I'd love it. But... Isn't this moving pretty fast?"

"In my experience, when an opportunity comes your way, you take it. You don't dither. You don't delay. If you do, next thing you know, it's slipped away." Her chin firmed. "I am not letting Charlie slip away. Oh sure, we could have a long-distance relationship, and that would probably work for a while. But I love being with him. I love his smile. I, well, I love him. He's good for me." She took Tara's hand in hers. "I haven't had a nightmare since I met him."

Tara thought back and, damn. She hadn't.

Though Tara didn't understand the wash of bitterness at her sister's words, she did get the peace surrounding her. Tina looked happier than she ever had.

So she hugged her and wished her well, but couldn't help thinking how unfair it all was. Things were so easy for Tina. Things were so clear.

She loved Charlie and wanted to spend her life with him.

Knowing Tina, it would all probably work out.

But for Tara, those things never worked out.

Never.

It just wasn't fair.

"Charlie and Tina are engaged." These were Tara's first words to Devlin when he stopped by the bakery on Thursday. Her pout was adorable. He wanted to kiss it off her face.

"I know. Isn't that great?"

She snorted and tossed her towel over her shoulder, locking the door behind him. She always locked the door behind him. As though she were expecting pirates to attack at three. "They're going away this weekend. To *Victoria*." She said it like it was Jupiter or something.

"I'm happy for them. Besides, it gives us the whole weekend together. Alone." He waggled his brow in what he hoped was an alluring fashion. She was not allured.

"Seriously? They've known each other two weeks!"

"According to Charlie, two weeks can seem like a lifetime."

"Oh brother." She stomped back behind the cases. He followed, nicking a cream puff from the refrigerated case.

"Come on Tara. Cut the kids some slack. They're young. They're in love. They want some time away…from us, I guess." He bit into the cream puff. Heaven.

She turned at his moan and glared at him. He counted himself lucky she hadn't snatched it from him and given him some gluten-free *carob* muffin instead. She'd lightened up on the gluten-free rampage over the last week, for which he was inordinately grateful. And her cream puffs were sinful.

"I think they're moving a little fast."

"It's their journey, Tara. They're grown ups."

"But—"

"They can make their own decisions about their lives." The irony, that he was saying these words about his brother, did not escape him.

"I know." She seemed to crumble. "It's just…"

"What?" He stepped closer and tugged her into his arms. She buried her face in his shirt. The dampness bespoke her tears. He tipped her chin up and wiped them away with a thumb, and then kissed her gently. "What is it, honey?"

She opened her mouth to respond but then her lips firmed and she gave her head a little shake and she pulled away. "Nothing."

But he knew it wasn't nothing.

A woman didn't cry because her sister was engaged.

A woman cried because her heart was aching.

Trouble was, he didn't know how to ease the pain. Or if he could.

"Look on the bright side. We have the whole weekend together. That is, if you don't have to work."

She glanced over her shoulder into the kitchen where Jose and another man were cleaning equipment and preparing for the next day's work. Devlin sketched a wave and Jose responded. "I don't have to work."

"Then let's go away too."

"I can't. I already made plans. Tina and I were going to go to the island. I already made arrangements with Kristi."

The island. That was doable. "Why don't you stay with me?"

You'd think he'd offered to fuck her naked on the beach, her expression was so mortified. "Stay at Ash's house? I couldn't."

"Why not?"

"Because the guys would lecture me. And probably kill you."

Damn. Visions of having her in his bed for two whole days—and nights—wafted away. From what he knew of her friends, they were very territorial. Even when it wasn't their territory.

"Can I see you then?"

She shot him a smile. And a wink. "If you keep your eyes open."

And while he knew and loved this playful mood, he recognized it for what it was.

She was keeping him at a distance.

Still. After all they'd shared.

He would allow it, but not for long.

He swallowed his frustration, bent his head and kissed her, appreciative when she stepped closer and nudged his crotch. It occurred to him that, at some point, he was going to need to dare her to give him a CPBJ right here in her bakery. Or maybe dare her to let him eat a cream puff off *her.*

Then something else occurred to him, absorbed him, consumed him. He pulled her closer and rubbed his crotch back and forth over her belly.

"What are you doing?" she hissed, glancing over her shoulder into the kitchen.

"You remember that Brazilian Wax you so brilliantly suggested?" he asked.

"Yeah."

"It itches."

CHAPTER NINETEEN

The next day he was miserable. For one thing, his crotch was on fire. For another, Tara called around three to tell him "something had come up and she couldn't make it after all." But, she added, he should go on to the island without her. The cool thread winding through her tone set his teeth on edge.

He'd pledged to be patient with her, and he had been. He'd thought he was making progress but the niggle of doubt he'd felt earlier widened into a gaping chasm.

Deep in the heart of his soul, he was worried.

Worried that she was slipping from his reach. That she was getting ready to dump him the way she'd dumped every guy before him.

To make things worse, when he got to Ash's place, he discovered he didn't have the house to himself. He recognized Parker's pristine roller in the foyer, and Richie's sloppy backpack next to it. He didn't mind Parker, but Richie was kind of an ass.

Maybe it was a good thing Tara wasn't coming. He didn't fancy spending the weekend with her…and Richie.

Figuring his friends were at Darby's, he dropped his bag on the hardwood floor next to the others, and headed out into the night. The bar was quiet for a Friday night, the lull before the weekend storm, but there were enough people there that he had to hunt for his friends. They were in the back, drinking whiskey and playing pool and chatting up two pretty blondes. Parker's face broke into a smile when he saw him and he waved. Richie was more boisterous.

"Devlin! My man!" he bellowed.

Apparently Richie had been drinking for a while.

Devlin sincerely hoped he wouldn't be cleaning up vomit this weekend. That would be the icing on his misery cake.

But he didn't want to think about cake. Cake made him think of bakers and that made him angry and impatient and sad. What he wanted was a drink. So when Parker called, "Come on over," Devlin did.

Richie waved to the two girls. And yes, they were girls. Co-eds. *Really, Richie?* "Meet Mia and Fransheene."

"Fran*cine*," the smaller one said, holding out her hand.

"This is Devlin Fox."

To his chagrin, their eyes lit up. "*The* Devlin Fox?" She spoke with a hint of a lisp, but he suspected it was affected.

"*Aw-thome.*" Oh holy crap. They *both* had speech impediments. God save him from almost-teenyboppers. "The guy from the internet?"

Yeah. He supposed that was where he was *from*.

Fransheene fluttered her lashes. "Ohmygod. You're like, totally famous."

"Only partially," he murmured, but no one got the joke.

Richie pointed at Charmaine, who was already on her way over, and bellowed, "Get this man a drink!"

He didn't want to wait. He picked up one of the shot glasses on the table and tossed it back and raised a finger to Charmaine for another.

Richie gaped at him. His lips worked. "Dude," he said. "That was Fransheene's drink.

"*Francine*," she said, and then she sidled up to Devlin and batted her lashes again. "But I don't mind sharing."

Egads. Was that her hand on his butt?

He sat down. Just so she had to let go of his ass. The foursome abandoned their game and joined him at the table. What followed was an awkward conversation about the trials and tribulations of college dorm life, and *like-grody-cafeteria-food* and *ohmygod-finals*. He tried to participate, but the banality of it all made his head spin. And his mind was beset with other things. Such as, had she really hesitated before she said "see you soon?" And that pause before "Something came up." Did that hint at a prevarication? It was difficult sifting through the swirling emotions and doubts and fear—especially with all the chirping in his ear.

He blew out a breath of relief when Mia and Fransheene announced to the assemblage that they were going to powder their noses. Also, Charmaine brought his next drink.

He tossed it back. The movement made him dizzy.

Parker cleared his throat. "You might want to slow down, buddy."

Richie snorted. "Parker, you're such a pussy." He leaned toward Devlin and hissed, "You really shouldn't have taken Francine's drink."

"Why not?" And why was his mouth filled with cotton wool?

Richie's lips parted, as though he was going to say something, but then glanced at Parker and blew out a laugh. "Oh, nothing, ass wipe. I *bought* it for her is all."

"Richie." When Parker frowned, he was really good at it. He was a lawyer after all. Devlin imagined there was call for him to frown with regularity. "Did you put something in that girl's drink?"

"What!" The word exploded from him and Richie slapped his chest with a palm. "I am wounded. Wounded I tell you."

"Goddamn it, Richie…"

"I didn't. I did not. I *swear.* May my cock and balls shrivel up and blow away if I'm lyin'."

"You better not be."

"I swear."

Devlin watched his exchange through a haze from afar. It was a nice afar. Warm and comfy and there wasn't any bothersome lingering trace of…whatever he'd been thinking about before.

And…Ah. Yeah. Right there. That felt nice.

He became aware that both Richie and Parker were staring at him.

"Whaa?" The 't' was too much effort, so he didn't bother.

"Devlin, why are you rubbing your crotch?" Parker's expression was a mixture of horror and amusement.

Devlin glanced down. Oh yeah. He was. It felt damn good. "It itches."

"Ahem." Sometimes Parker was such a…*lawyer.* "And why does your crotch itch?"

"Did some bitch give you crabs?" Richie waggled his brows.

Devlin frowned. "None of your beeswax why it itches." And then he winced at his own unintended pun.

Wax?

Never again.

He caught a glimpse of the lisp sisters heading back to the table, giggling, and he grimaced. "I think I'm going to sit at the bar."

"Dude. You can't leave me," Parker whispered.

Devlin clapped him on the shoulder. It took a couple tries. "You made your bed, dude. Lie in it. I'm going over there." He notched his head toward the bar where Charmaine was drying glasses.

He stood, a difficulty, but he managed, and made his way across the room, relieved to finally reach a stool. He sat and tendered a smile. "Hey."

Her response was a little cooler. "Hey."

"Whiskey?"

She raised a brow, but gave him a healthy pour. Her gaze flickered down. "I see you're dressed today."

He grinned. Didn't know why it was funny, but it was. "Yeah." He shrugged. "So far. But there's always hope."

She snorted a laugh and resumed her work.

It was a nice, peaceful silence with absolutely no lisping. Still, he broke it. "My brother just got engaged."

She shifted his drink so she could wipe the counter, though he clearly hadn't spilled anything. That would be a tradgey. A tradagy. A tragedy. Yeah. A tragedy.

"That seems like a reason to celebrate. Not drink yourself silly."

"I'm not silly." But he was. "My love life isn't going well." Mortifying to admit something like that to someone he barely knew, but guys did that in bars. Didn't they?

"Really?" Her lips twisted. "Is this the same chick who left you bare-assed naked out behind the bar?"

"Um. Yes?"

"And it's not going well. Imagine that."

"She has commitment issues."

Charmaine blew out a breath. "Who doesn't?"

"Me."

She studied him for a minute. "Look, you seem like a decent guy…"

"I am a decent guy."

"You deserve a woman who wants to be with you as much as you want to be with her. If this chick isn't into it, quit torturing yourself.

There are a million fish in the sea." She swept out her arm to encompass the bar, which was practically devoid of women at the moment. But that didn't negate her point. There were a million women in the sea. A billion, probably. Well not *in* the sea, *per se*. In the metaphorical sea. But there were fish. And there were seas. And they wanted to be together…

Okay. Maybe he'd had a bit too much to drink. Point being, there were probably a million women who would want to be with him more than Tara did.

The thought did not comfort him.

He didn't want a million women.

He wanted Tara.

"Damn it. I love her."

Charmaine stilled. "You love her? The woman who stole your jeans and left you standing naked in the cold night?"

"S'wasn't that cold." He tossed back his shot, surprised to discover the glass was empty. And then, after a moment. "Yes. I do. Love her."

"Have you told her you love her?"

"Oh, hell no. I couldn't do that."

She blew out another sigh, which made her bangs fluff up in a rather fascinating way. His eyes crossed, all on their own, as he fixated on it. "You have to tell her. It's very important."

"Can't. She doesn't like mooners."

"Ah… Mooners?"

"You know. Guys who moon. Who get all clingy and shit."

"Ah. That kind of mooner. I was confused."

"You were?"

"This *is* the woman who stole your pants, after all, and left you bare assed naked next to a dumpster."

Apparently, judging from her smirk, she was saying something clever, but Devlin couldn't follow her train of thought. He shook his head to clear it which was a big mistake because then everything went all swirly and the room shifted. Gravity started tugging him to the right.

"Are you okay?" she asked from very far away.

"I'm fine."

"Maybe you should lie down. Darby has a couch in his office. Do you promise not to throw up?"

"Throw up?" An excellent notion. The bar was lunging like a ferry in heavy chop.

"Oh, God. Here." She set something before him. A glass full of air. No. Wait. Water. "Drink this."

He did what she asked because it seemed like good advice. While he emptied the glass—which tasted phenomenal, by the way—she came around the bar and hooked her arm around his waist, mercifully keeping him from collapsing on the floor.

"How much have you had?"

He held up three fingers.

"Lordy. You don't drink much, do you?"

He attempted to focus on her face. It was a challenge. If only she would quit moving. "Nope."

"You are ass over elbows too. Come on."

"Where are we going?"

"To lie down."

"Excellent." Tara didn't want him. Not the way he wanted to be wanted. But there were a million fish who would love to swim in his ocean. Or something like that. He attempted to shoot Charmaine a sexy leer. Perhaps it wasn't terribly sexy because she pursed her lips, and not in a *kiss-me* kind of way. In a *lemony* kind of way.

As he stood, he teetered, and grabbed hold of her for ballast.

That he grabbed her boob was not intentional.

Or maybe it was.

She sent him a scorching glare. "Don't. Even. Think about it," she snapped, removing his hand. "I've maimed men for less."

He winced as he remembered who she was. Remembered the time she'd dumped a pot of coffee on him when he'd gotten out of line. Thank God it hadn't been too hot. The memory sobered him. A little.

"Sorry." She was really nice. And she was helping him stay off the floor. Which was also nice. As much as he liked sawdust on a bar floor, he didn't like it in his nostrils. "Thank you."

She sighed. "You're welcome. Now come on. Let's get you into the back. I have work to do."

He only stumbled a couple times as they made their way across the hard planking. When they reached the office door she paused. "You should tell her, you know."

Devlin blinked. "Tell her what?"

"Tell her that you love her, silly. That's the only way you'll know for sure if she wants you or not."

"But what if she walks away?" God. He couldn't bear the thought. "What if she cuts me loose?" Like every other guy she'd ever dated.

Charmaine tipped her head up and smiled at him. It was a soft, sad smile. "Then you'll know it wasn't meant to be, I suppose. Wouldn't you rather know for sure?"

No. "I suppose."

"Of course you do. Besides, she may surprise you. She may feel the same way for you."

"Do you think?"

He probably imagined that look of pity in her eye. "Anything is possible. Who knows what she's really thinking unless you ask."

It all sounded very logical and profound. Devlin hoped he could remember it in the morning. Still, Charmaine's words filled him with a giddy, ridiculous hope. "Thank you." He bent down and pulled her into a hug. She allowed it, and even hugged him back. It was a nice, comfortable hug. He could probably sleep here. But something *un*comfortable pinged in his crotch at the contact.

What was it?

Oh yeah.

Itchy.

His crotch was itchy.

He probably shouldn't have rubbed it against her.

She yanked back with a snarl. Without her support he nearly teetered to the floor. "Sorry," he slurred. "Didn't mean to do that but I had an itch to scratch."

"I see that." Her tone was dry as dust.

"Not that kind of itch," he felt compelled to explain as she guided him into an office cluttered with boxes and fishing lures and—thankfully—a sofa. He was getting wobblier and woozier by the moment. "She made me get a Brazilian Wax and it itches like hell."

Charmaine gaped at him. "She made you get a Brazilian?"

"Hurt like the very devil."

"I can imagine." As she settled him onto the sofa, she tried to nibble her amusement away and failed. "Why ever did she make you do that?"

He grinned. It was probably a little lopsided. "Simple," he said as she tucked a small pillow beneath his head. "I lost a bet."

And that was the last thing he remembered for a long, long while.

When he woke up, it was morning, his head was throbbing and all he could think was, *"As God is my witness, I will never drink whiskey again."*

CHAPTER TWENTY

All right. She was a coward. She admitted it. She shouldn't have canceled on Devlin. But as she'd watched Tina getting ready for her weekend with Charlie, humming to herself as she packed— *humming*—panic had descended.

Tina was in love. In love. And happy. She was ready to leave her career behind and commit herself to a man, one man, for the rest of her life. And she seemed *happy* about it. Deliriously happy.

The anticipation and hope on her sister's face lanced Tara to the core.

Because it was a familiar look.

It was a look she saw often in the mirror as she prepared for a date with Devlin.

That realization, of course, had led to another horrifying epiphany. Her feelings for Devlin were far too strong. She'd never wanted to be with a man, never enjoyed being with a man quite like this. She'd certainly never craved a man like this.

And the really scary thought? It wasn't sex she craved. It was his smile, the sound of his voice, his laugh.

Stupid stuff like that.

When had this happened? How had she let him seep under her skin?

She'd always been able to keep a man at arm's length. Until now.

And it terrified her.

So she'd called and canceled.

It wasn't until Tina and Charlie were gone, and she was left alone in her empty apartment, that the hollowness hit her. Her life was a void. A meaningless string of pointless encounters. Even her bakery, which had always been the joy of her existence—ceased to excite her.

Her passion for her work had been an illusion. A construct to occupy her time, her emotion, her attention. A distraction to help her forget what she really wanted, needed. Craved. She saw that now. A bakery couldn't love you back or hold you or kiss you. Or keep you warm at night.

Devlin could.

Oh, could he.

And she missed him. Even though they'd had lunch today, she missed him.

Shit.

She was going to have to cave.

Grumbling to herself, she tossed some things into a bag and raced to the docks to catch the last ferry. She barely made it. The ride over, which she usually enjoyed, especially in the evening, was a blur. She tried to focus on the passing scenery, all shadowed and speckled with the sparkling lights on the shore, but her mind kept drifting to *him.* Something he'd said or done or tried to get her to do. More than once, the memory ended with her grinning like a loon.

By the time the ferry docked, she was in a wad.

She walked to Lane's house—now her house too, since she'd signed the infamous lease—and dropped her bag in the foyer. Her plan was to head straight over to Ash's place, where Devlin was staying, but Kristi, who was walking through the kitchen with a mug in her hand, caught sight of her and waved. "Tara!" she called. "You made it."

"Hey Kristi." Instead of escaping, as she wanted to do, and running into the arms of the man she—well, into Devlin's arms, she stepped into the hall. "What'cha doin'?"

Kristi laughed and nodded at Cam, who was snoozing on the sofa. "Nothing. Wanna watch a movie?"

No. She didn't. "I, ah, thought I'd go to Darby's."

Kristi's eyes glimmered. "To Darby's?"

"Yeah." She looked down and fiddled with the hem of her shirt. "Or next door. Devlin might be there."

"Hmm." Kristi took a sip of her drink. Cocoa, judging from the pouf of whipped cream on her nose. "Do you want me to go with you?"

"You don't have to."

"I don't mind. You probably shouldn't be wandering around alone at night."

"It's safe here."

"I know. But I'd feel better if we came with you."

"We?"

Kristi nudged Cam awake. "Wh-what?" he sputtered.

"Get up. We're going to Darby's."

"I thought we were staying in."

"Tara's here. We're going to Darby's."

"Or next door," she murmured under her breath. But they both missed it.

"Hookay." Cam heaved himself off the sofa and got ready to go. And for Cam, the process of getting ready to go consisted of brushing off his shirt. "Let's hit it."

It was a nice, moonlit night, so the path was clear. "I really didn't need company," she said, flicking a quick glance at Ash's house as they passed. It was dark. Okay. Maybe the bar was a good idea after all.

The lights of town appeared in the distance. Music and laughter and the crack of a pool shot reached out to greet them. As they neared, butterflies arose to clash in her belly. Seriously? Who knew butterflies could be so violent.

And why she was so nervous, she had no clue.

There was no reason to be nervous. None at all. She was going to Darby's with her friends—something she'd done a thousand times—and she *might* see a guy she knew.

Lordy. Definitely nervous.

She stepped inside and scanned the crowd. She saw Devlin's friends in the back with two women, but of Devlin there was no—

There he was. On the other side of the restaurant by the bar.

Her heart leaped. Then thudded once. Then seized.

Devlin wasn't alone. He was talking to Charmaine, leaning in close. Too close for a casual conversation.

Then he hugged her. Hugged her tight.

And if that weren't horrifying enough, he rubbed against her like a jungle cat in heat.

Charmaine pulled away and then led him into the shadows, into a back room.

The door closed behind them.

"Tara? Tara, honey, are you okay?" She was vaguely aware of Kristi's presence at her side. She tried to make a noise, but it came out like a wheeze. She was paralyzed. Pole axed. Devastated.

How could he? How *could* he?

Oh, a nasty voice in the back of her head mocked, *he could.* They'd never made a commitment to each other. Never promised to be monogamous. The topic had never even come up.

Casual sex. Fuck buddies. No relationship. No strings attached.

What idiocy.

She didn't understand the hot wind whipping through her. Or the red tide clouding her vision. Was utterly unfamiliar with the sudden blinding urge to snatch a blonde-headed bitch bald. But she knew what it was, this emotion.

It was jealousy. And it was fierce.

"We need to go. Now." Kristi, again, from the fog.

"What?" Cam squawked. "But we just got here."

Kristi ignored him and put her arm around Tara, leading her back into the shadows of the night. Tara followed, because she couldn't not. Couldn't even function without her guidance. Behind them, she heard Cam blow out a breath and mutter, "Oh, all right."

And that was the last word any of them spoke until they reached the house.

"Here you go. This will make you feel better." Kristi thrust a mug at her. Tara stared at the pouf of whipped cream.

"It's cocoa." Cocoa wouldn't make her feel better.

"I know."

"I wanted gin."

"Try this first. It will warm you. You're like ice." She was cold. She didn't know why, except for the fact that her heart had frozen up like a Popsicle.

Obediently, she sipped. Warmth flooded her, but not enough to defrost that wedge of ice in her chest.

"Isn't it yummy?" Kristi was a firm believer in the recuperative powers of hot chocolate. Apparently, she'd never tried gin.

"Mmm."

"Oh, Tara. I am so sorry," she said, dropping down on the sofa beside her.

She'd sent Cam out to the lone grocery store on the island to pick up some coffee. He'd thrown up his hands and muttered, "We just got back," but he'd gone. And they were alone.

"I'm okay. Really." If she ignored the tear trying to escape the corner of her eye, maybe Kristi wouldn't notice.

She did, and dabbed it with a thumb. "He's a jerk. You're better off without him."

Tara sighed. "It's not his fault, Kristi."

"What do you mean it's not his fault? I saw what was going on there. You can't deny what we saw." She didn't add, *what's happening right now in the back room of Darby's Bar and Grill*, but it skulked behind her words.

Tara pretended her shudder was from the cold and took another sip of cocoa. "We don't have an understanding."

"What do you mean?"

"We don't have an understanding. He's free as a bird. Free to do as he pleases…" The horror of that thought racked her. She should have pinned him down. At least a little.

Kristi shook her head and wrapped her arms around Tara's shoulder. "Oh, honey."

"It's okay. Really it is." She hiccupped and then realized it was a sob.

"It doesn't look okay. Do you…"

Tara sniffed. "Do I what?"

"Do you have feelings for him?"

Such a simple question should not cause her to puddle up so, but it did. Before she knew it, tears were falling and falling hard. One fat drop landed on her hand and she brushed it away.

"Do you?"

"K-kind of."

"And are you going to let that waitress have him?"

Tara blinked at the fervor in Kristi's voice. "What can I do? He's a grown up. He can do what he wants…"

Kristi sprang to her feet. "For heaven's sake woman, if you really like him, you have to fight for him. You have to go over there and tell him that you want him, that you want something more from him.

You have to *tell* him. You have to show him."

"Show him?" Tara asked plaintively. She peeped at Kristi over the lip of her mug as she took a sip of her cocoa. A pouf of whipped creamed clung to her nose. "How?"

Kristi quirked a brow and sent her a naughty smile. "How do you think?"

CHAPTER TWENTY-ONE

As determined as she was, it was still mid-morning before Tara could drum up the courage to go next door and face Devlin. For one thing, she was an out-and-out coward. For another, she slept in. She hadn't slept well the night before, tossing and turning and agonizing over how to tell him that she wanted more than just casual sex.

He hadn't asked for anything more. Hadn't pushed for a commitment of any kind. Hadn't even opened that door. When she'd suggested he work off his debt to her with meaningless casual encounters, he'd simply agreed.

Never once had he given her any indication that he wanted a relationship beyond their dare dates which, if one were completely honest with oneself, were nothing more than incredibly satisfying and occasionally outrageous booty calls.

Would he balk if she asked for more?

Could she survive that?

There was only one way to find out.

So, steeling her spine, she marched over to the house next door and knocked. When no one answered, she nearly turned tail and scampered away. She reminded herself to be brave and knocked again. Louder.

Her heart skipped a beat when she heard heavy footsteps approach. But then, when the door swung open to reveal one of his friends—and the creepy one to boot, grinning like a loon—it sank.

"Well hello there baby." *Blech.* She hated when guys called her baby.

"Yeah. Hi. Is Devlin here?"

The creep raised his arm and leaned against the doorjamb. "Devlin? What do you want with Devlin, sweet thang?" Really? A twang? Did that work? Ever?

"I would like to talk to him."

He offered an oily smile. "Well, come on in. I'm Richie, by the way."

She grunted in response and followed him into the house, trying not to think about the last time she'd been there. She bit her lip as they passed the spot where she and Devlin had tangled for the very first time. There. Up against the wall.

Surprisingly, there were no scorch marks.

They emerged from the hall into the airy great room and Tara glanced around. It was empty. "Where's Devlin?"

Richie strode to the bar and pulled out two glasses. "Let me make you a drink."

A drink? "It's not even noon."

He shrugged and opened a bottle and sloshed two fingers into each glass. "Just one drink. Don't be such a party pooper."

Oh. Was this a party? "No drink. I need to talk to Devlin. Where is he?"

Richie prowled across the room toward her. She took the proffered glass and set it on the table. He frowned at her and licked his lips and, for some unfathomable reason, leaned in way too close. "He's not here. But I am."

Comprehension dawned as a pair of fishy lips hovered nearer. Tara's hand shot out and wedged against his chest, forcing him back.

"Hey baby. Don't be so cold." He pushed against her hand, looming.

"Don't call me baby. And back off, buster."

He didn't. In fact, he advanced. "Come on, baby. You get the picture. A hot number like you coming by, dressed all sexy and shit. Looking for a man. And here I am."

"I'm looking for Devlin. Where is he?"

Richie shrugged. "Who knows. He didn't come home last night."

Her heart plummeted at that. He must have spent the night…with *her.*

"Don't look so sad. You must know Devlin will fuck anything in a skirt." He laughed and edged to the side, boxing her in. He reached around to tug on her ponytail.

"Quit it."

"It's not like you're his woman. Besides, I'm just tryin' to be friendly, baby. "

Friendly?

Friendly was *not* forcibly backing her up against the wall. Friendly was *not* grabbing her boob.

Also, friendly was not goring a guy in the nuts with a sharp knee, but she did it anyway.

His eyes crossed and he doubled over, wheezing like a rusty bellows. "Jesus, woman. What the fuck did you do that for?"

"I am his woman, *baby*. And when I tell you to back off, back the fuck off."

"What the fuck is going on here?"

Relief hit her like a tsunami as Devlin's irate bellow shook the room. She whirled around to face him and—

And he looked like hell.

"Devlin."

"Tara." He opened his arms and she went to him. She had to step over Richie's prostrate form to get to him, but she did. And damn, it was nice being in his arms again. "Richie, what the fuck did you do?"

"Nothin'." The douche picked himself up off the ground, adjusted his dented package and glared at her.

Devlin growled. A little. "Did he hurt you?" He stroked her hair.

"No."

He glowered at his friend. "Good. You get to live."

"Jesus, Dev, don't be such a—"

"Out."

"What?" A warble.

"Get. Out. Get. Out. Now."

Something in Devlin's tone must have resonated in his meaty skull, because Richie did just that. He grumbled and muttered as he made his way up the stairs, but he left. Thank God.

"You have the worst taste in friends," she said.

Devlin snorted. "He's not *my* friend." Then his gaze fixed on her. "Did you mean what you said?"

She tapped her lip, as though trying to recall. "What did I say?"

"That you're my woman." She liked the way his voice dropped an octave, rumbled through her.

"Maybe."

He blinked. "Maybe?"

"Did you spend the night with Charmaine?"

His lips opened and closed. "No. I slept on Darby's couch. I had way too much to drink... Why would you think I stayed with Charmaine?"

"I saw you two together. Last night. At the bar."

His brow wrinkled. "Oh. Yeah. She helped me into the office. Did I mention I had too much to drink?"

"And that was it? That was all?"

"Not exactly."

Her belly flipped. "What else?"

"She gave me some advice."

Tara pulled back and studied him. "Advice?"

"Mmm hmm."

"What did she say?"

"She told me I should tell you."

"T-tell me what?"

He swallowed and sucked in a deep breath. "She told me I should tell you how much I lo— like you..."

Her heart leaped, danced at his near slip. She knew what he'd been going to say. She could see it in his eyes. It didn't bother her that he wasn't ready to say the words yet. She wasn't ready to hear them. She certainly wasn't ready to admit she might feel the same. But she was close.

To admitting it.

"Oh?" She sidled closer and fingered the neckline of his t-shirt. "And how much do you lo— like me?"

A grin broke on his face. "A lot. A really, really a lot." Their gazes met and tangled. And heat rose. "So..." He nibbled his lip. "Did you mean what you said? About being my woman?"

"I did." She peeped up at him. "Does that make you feel uncomfortable?

"Uncomfortable?"

"I know you dislike being tied down as much me."

"I kind of like being tied down with you."

"You...do?"

"I wouldn't mind being tied down *by* you as well, but that's a whole other discussion."

She snorted a laugh. "That would be pretty awesome."

"You are pretty awesome." His Adam's apple worked. "But I... I would like...more with you."

"What?"

"You heard what I said. Don't start retreating."

"I'm not retreating." But she was. She could feel it. She closed her eyes and sucked in a breath and pushed the old fear away.

It was time for an entirely new fear.

"I will probably always be a little...skittish."

His hold on her tightened. "I know. I understand. But Tara, we deserve a chance. What we have is something special."

"I know." It was. It was something worth exploring.

"So will you do it? Will you give us a try?"

"Yes."

"Yes?" She never expected such a look of joy at so simple a declaration.

"For real? As in a relationship? A real live relationship? With strings and everything?"

She nodded and bit her tongue to keep from making a joke about ropes as well. This was probably not a good time to be flippant.

"Say it."

"Yes. I will be your girlfriend."

"Woo hoo!" he whooped and swung her up in his arms and twirled her around. "You are my girlfriend."

She laughed because he said it in a sing-song voice.

And then her heart thudded hard, because he set her down and leaned closer. His playful expression changed into something hot and intense. "Prove it," he said. "Go on. I dare you."

EPILOGUE

"What are you doing?"

Devlin's fingers froze over the keyboard as a soft, warm, fragrant presence wrapped itself around him. He leaned back into her, unable to stop his grin. He'd dared her to prove she was his girlfriend, and man, did that woman take her dares seriously. She'd nearly *girlfriended* him to death. It had been awesome. Afterwards she'd fallen asleep, and while he'd wanted more, he'd decided she needed her rest. So he'd padded naked over to the desk to do a little work and ended up deleting some old photos from his phone. He didn't want them. Not anymore.

"What am I doing?"

"Umm hmm."

He tapped in a few words. "Right now?"

"Of course right now."

"I'm writing a review."

"Blech. Don't you ever stop?"

He spun around in his chair to face her and barked a laugh. She was wearing his jeans. They were way too big. And obstructed the view. He tugged them off and pulled her into his lap. Her silky skin rubbed against his. He couldn't help but explore…a little. "I like writing reviews."

"Do ya?" She kissed him. Her mouth was delectable.

"I do."

She ran her palm over his cheek and up to his forehead, riffling his hair. She studied him and frowned.

"What?"

She shrugged. "I dunno. There was a flicker when you said that."

"A flicker?"

"Yeah. Like you almost didn't believe it. Or you were trying to convince yourself it's true."

Damn. She was observant when she wanted to be. "I love writing reviews."

Her brow arched. "Flicker."

"I do…" Her scrutiny of him was ruthless. "Okay. Don't get me wrong, I do love what I do but…"

"But?"

"But don't you ever dream about doing something more important? Something meaningful?"

She shrugged. "Pastries *are* important and meaningful."

"This is true." He knew better than to argue with her on that point. "But I was speaking metaphorically."

"Ah. Metaphorically. So you meant 'you' as in *you*."

His smile might have been a little sheepish. "Okay. Yeah."

"Well, what kind of meaningful and important thing do you dream of doing?"

"I don't know." He pulled her closer and tucked her head into his shoulder. She toyed with his chest hair in a most distracting way. "My brother did something very important. He joined the Army. Fought for our country. Sacrificed his legs for national security. And I… I write pointless reviews."

"They're hardly pointless."

He grunted. "It doesn't seem like a good balance somehow."

"Hmm."

He tipped his head to glance down at her, intrigued by her tone. "What?"

She kissed the underside of his chin once, twice, three times. As though she wanted to do that all day. "I think you already know what kind of important and significant thing you want to do."

He liked the way she curled around him and nestled in, his girlfriend. It gave him…ideas. "This meaningful and important thing, might it involve your tongue and a gallon of peanut butter?"

She smacked him, but gently. "Quit retreating."

"I'm not."

"You are. You know what it is, this other thing you want to do. If you've dreamed of it, you know what it is."

Heat rose in his cheeks. "I do. But…"

"But what?"

"I'm embarrassed to say."

"So it does involve peanut butter…"

He couldn't help but laugh. "No. It's writing. But…" He dipped his head, unable to look her in the eye. "I think I would like to try writing a novel."

When she didn't laugh, he peeped at her.

She wasn't staring at him bug-eyed, which was encouraging, so he looked her full on.

And when she smiled and said, in a very serious tone, "Devlin, I think that would be wonderful," he knew—*simply knew*—she was the one for him.

And he was the one for her.

Forever.

He pulled her close for a kiss. When it ended, they were both breathless.

"God, Devlin," she sighed, nuzzling deeper into his embrace.

He stroked her back. "I know."

"It just feels so…right."

"I know."

She peeped up at him, her adorable face wreathed in worry. "I'm scared."

He pressed his lips to her forehead. "I know. But I'm here. We'll work through all of it together. Okay?"

Even though she nodded, she nibbled her lower lip, the tell for her hidden doubt. She fixated on his chin, riffling his scruff with her fingers. She pressed a little kiss on the underside. "I don't know what I would do if…"

Yeah. He knew what she was thinking. *If they didn't work out.* "That's not going to happen." Not if he had a damn thing to say about it. "We're gonna be great, Tara. We're gonna be awesome. Forever."

He didn't intend for that last little word to escape, but it did. He stilled, studied her, gauging her response.

That it was a smile, a rapturous smile, filled his heart with joy.

"Forever?" An awestruck whisper, as though she'd never dared contemplate such a thing.

"Yup. As long as you want me, I'll be here. You're stuck with me."

Her tentative demeanor became certain. And mischievous. "Oh, I'll probably want you for a while."

"I'm gratified."

"At least twenty years or so." She shifted, deliberately. His cock stirred.

"O-only twenty?"

She shrugged. "Maybe more."

"Hmm. That many years… Seems like a challenge."

The glint in her eye set his blood aflame. "Do you think you can handle it?"

"Maybe."

She wiggled on his lap.

Or…maybe not. At least, not without tipping her, ass over elbows, and sinking deep.

"Well, Devlin Fox," she quipped, slipping off his lap and onto her knees before him. "I dare you to try."

ABOUT THE AUTHOR

Her Royal Hotness, Sabrina York, is the New York Times and USA Today Bestselling author of hot, humorous stories for smart and sexy readers. Her titles range from sweet & sexy to scorching romance. Visit her webpage at www.sabrinayork.com to check out her books, excerpts and contests.

BOOKS BY SABRINA YORK

Tryst Island Series—Steamy Contemporary Romance
Rebound, Book 1
Dragonfly Kisses, Book 2
Smoking Holt, Book 3
Heart of Ash, Book 4
Devlin's Dare, Book 5
Parker's Passion, Book 6

Anthologies and Collections
Five Alarm Fire (High Octane Heroes)
A Cowboy for Delilah (Cowboy Heat)
Saving Charlotte (Smokin' Hot Firemen)
Stone Hard Seal (Hot Alpha Seals: Military Romance Megaset)
Whipped (Brought to his Knees Collection)

Short Stories/Novellas
Extreme Couponing, Fierce, Pushing Her Buttons, Man Hungry,
Rising Green (Horror), Training Tess, Trickery

Wired Series—Steamy Contemporary Romance
Adam's Obsession, Book 1
Tristan's Temptation, Book 2
Making Over Maris, Book 3

Noble Passions Series—Steamy Regency
Folly, Book 1
Dark Fancy, Book 2
Dark Duke, Book 3
Brigand, Book 4
Defiant, Book 5

Fantasy (Romance)
Lust Eternal